I0746282

Pisgah Press was established in 2011 to publish and promote works of quality offering original ideas and insight into the human condition, the realm of knowledge, and the world around us.

Copyright © 2024 Jeffrey Melvin Hutchins
Printed in the United States of America

Published by Pisgah Press, LLC
PO Box 9663, Asheville, NC 28815
www.pisgahpress.com

Book & cover design: A.D. Reed, Pisgah Press, LLC

Library of Congress Cataloging-in-Publication Data
Hutchins, Jeffrey Melvin
Perpetuonics: A Novel/Hutchins

Library of Congress Control Number: 2024945620

ISBN: 978-1-942016-91-5
Fiction

First Edition
First Printing
October 2024

PERPETUONICS

A Novel

Jeffrey Melvin Hutchins

Pisgah Press, LLC
Asheville, NC
www.pisgahpress.com

ACKNOWLEDGEMENTS

Creativity is, paradoxically, an intensely private pursuit and a necessarily communal one.

Therefore, I could not have completed *Perpetuonics* without the generous and wise support of many people. I must acknowledge and venerate those who read this manuscript in its many different versions:

Howard Belfor	Mike Czeczot
Diane Hutchins	Rachel Hutchins
Toby Ives	John Edward King
Nell Hutchins Shapiro	Danee Sullivan
Michael Taeger	Jack Williams

I also thank my wonderful family members who encouraged me to keep going on this project:

Bobby Duncan	Daniel Shapiro
Greg Hutchins	Valerie LePine

If you, dear reader, are searching these acknowledgements in vain for your own name, then please forgive me. You are one of many unnamed who deserve my hearty thanks for your friendship, for your love, and for your good spirit.

Thanks to Andy Reed of Pisgah Press for his guidance and support.

THIS BOOK IS DEDICATED TO

Diane, Rachel, Nell,
Bobby, Daniel,
Theo, Charlie
and
Denton the Dragon

PERPETUONICS

A Novel

This Product Made by Human Intelligence

PROLOGUE

"All utopias are dystopias."

— A.E. Samaan

The Dingdom. That's what I named the world in which Digital beINGS—"Dings"—exist. I'm Declan Marchand, the founder of perpetuonics, the technology that converts living people into digital beings. They are no longer alive, nor are they exactly dead. The bodies they once inhabited are most certainly gone, but their thoughts and memories and emotions—their souls, if you wish—continue to function.

Dings are technically called abliving, i.e., "away from living."

A Ding can do everything now that they did when alive, except operate a body. They can think and learn and feel emotions. They can feel emotional pain, but not physical pain. They can remember everything they knew from their earliest memories to the moment their brains were collected and stored on computer servers.

The only gap in their memories is the time between their collection and when their Ding is activated, which occurs only after their living body dies. That gap could be as little as a day or as long as several decades. A person can pay a great amount to be collected as often as they want, but a perpetuonics company is obliged, by law, to preserve only one collection per person.

When a person who has been collected dies, their body is disposed of the same way bodies are always processed: burial, cremation, composting, etc. That process does not affect their digital being.

A Ding can communicate with living people or with other Dings, although they are subject to rules and restrictions, of course.

Not every Living wants or can afford to be collected. In becoming a Ding, someone is saying, "I want to outlive my physical body. I want my soul to go on, presumably forever."

PART ONE
Evolution

"Eternity is not something that begins after you are dead.
We are in it now."

—Charlotte Perkins Gilman

Chapter 1

"I hate being human. I wish I were … something else," I said, as I carefully assembled two turkey-and-Swiss on rye sandwiches in my too-small kitchen in my too-small Cambridge flat. It was the first time I had put into words the thoughts that had been percolating for months, afraid to speak aloud. Now that the thoughts had form, my thirty-six-year-old body felt relief and elation.

"What are you talking about, Declan?" Dar asked me. Her parents—well, her father, a biologist—had named her Darwina, a name she forbade anyone ever to use. She had even shortened it on the family tree her brother, Mendel, kept. At forty-two, Mendel was seven years older than Dar, whom I had been dating off and on since we met at Boston University.

"Extra-human. I want to be extra-human," I said.

"What does that even mean?" She brushed her walnut-brown hair from the side of her face. "I don't get why you're bringing this up."

I paused to find the words. "I like having a human body. I'm grateful for all it does. Like when I had Covid-36, I couldn't think my way out of it. I couldn't wish it away. I needed my immune system to work to save me. So, while I appreciate that my body keeps my brain alive, I think it's kind of holding me back."

"Have you been snorting something?" Dar looked confused.

"No. Think about it … Look how we socialize, most of us, anyway. We join groups of people who look like us, are about our age, go to the same school or church or job, and who will vote like us. Our thoughts are not our thoughts, because we probably heard them from someone else first, or read them in the same journals our friends are reading."

Dar was annoyed. "I'm not like that."

"Yeah, you are, but that's not my point." I didn't dare let Dar get a word in here or I'd lose the momentum I could feel blitzing my body. "There are other people who look a lot like me, but otherwise we're nothing alike. My body and face and scraggly beard aren't me."

"Then who've I been sleeping with?"

I laughed, and Dar did, too.

'Well, yeah, bodies are good for some things, but even that proves what I'm trying to say. Our need for sex has ruined more damn lives."

Dar huffed, "It's about to ruin yours, that's for sure."

I ignored her empty threat. We always talked with each other like we were in a sitcom. "Look at President Clinton fifty years ago. Look at all those Catholic priests and gymnastics coaches when we were in high school. Look at that governor what's his name from last year? Simon?"

"All men, I might point out," she said.

"Yeah," I conceded, "but women have their problems, too. Like having to give birth and to nurture helpless babies ..."

"And to put up with assholes who hit on us."

"Right! See? That's what I'm saying. Bodies are inconvenient. We'd be better off if we didn't have them. Think about all the time you spend doing stupid, repetitive stuff, like washing dishes, doing laundry, making sandwiches ..." I took a bite of mine.

"Cleaning toilets," she added.

"Right. Wouldn't it be great if you never had to do that stuff again?"

"And pooping! Ohmigod, flossing. It's so boring and gross,

and my gums always bleed."

"Have you seen a dentist?" That was, apparently, not the right response.

"Fuck off. Of course, I go to the dentist," Dar said.

"Sorry. I knew that. Anyway, that's not the point either. I have an idea so we'll never have to clean a toilet or floss our teeth or do our laundry ever again."

"Sounds like we're dead."

I gave her a hard stare. "Kinda."

I could not know then that I would end up as a spy for a man who wouldn't be born for fifty years.

Chapter 2

Four years later, in 2045, my prototype was ready, thanks to advances in brain-mapping technology, artificial intelligence, and quantum computing. Dar was teaching ESL in Unified Korea. I missed her like crazy, but her absence freed me to work night and day on my project.

Twibil Biotech, a cutting-edge company from the early twenty-first century, had backed my research, given me office space in Cambridge, a powerful new Quantumac™, and paid me enough as a contractor so I could move to the first floor of a large house about two kilometers from the office. Now they were ready to spin off a subsidiary company: Twibil Perpetuonics. First, though, they wanted a demonstration, which meant I had a lot of work to do to get there.

I planned two phases of the roll-out. First, I would create an entirely digital being—a Ding, as I called it. I built the first Ding from scratch, meaning I wrote all the code for an imaginary person. I pored over a dozen psychology books trying to determine everything I would need to create a "personality." Creating a "male" seemed easier to me, I guess because I could relate better to a guy, so I created Cody.

Also in Phase 1, I employed quantum mechanics and A.I. to create virtual vision. Dings must be able to see and process images the same way humans can. They would be able to "see" any stored or live image. I developed an AI interface that could translate any visual image, moving or still, into code that Cody could process. It's the same way a human brain converts light waves into usable content. I can look at a tree, see it consistently the same way each time, understand what it is, and instantly make thousands of decisions about it: its color, its name, how old it might be, how tall it is, what season of the year it must be, etc. Dings will need that same ability. I wanted Cody to be able to see me talking to him through a live camera.

Cody was a disappointment to me. When I activated him, he worked, but barely. There were too many gaps in his background. He had too few memories. I had given him a backstory, but it was dreadfully insufficient, and his reactions to various stimuli were not at all what I wanted.

My friends thought I was building a robot. When I brought Jey and Lisa to my tiny lab in Cambridge, they expected to see a machine, something with appendages and an ability to interact with its environment. Instead, all they saw was a computer screen and a set of speakers sitting on my beat-up second-hand desk that I had tidied up for the occasion.

"So, where's this robot you've been working on?" Lisa asked. She had turned thirty a couple of weeks before, and we had been out celebrating her engagement to Jey. I mentioned Cody to them, and they were excited when I told them that no one had ever met Cody before. They wanted to be the first. Their excitement motivated me to finish Cody 1.0. I had to work about sixteen hours a day, but I got it done a couple of hours before they arrived.

Lisa was a physical therapist. She was petite and curvy, in great condition. Her arms were lean and strong. She usually wore colorful shirts with cap sleeves, which were once again in fashion. Her short blond hair, often accented in green or blue, stopped an inch above her shoulders. I had befriended Lisa when she worked on me after my bike accident, when a car brushed my back wheel and then sped off.

"There is no robot," I said. "Cody is a Ding. That's a

portmanteau of Digital beING. Cody, I want you to meet my friends Lisa and Jey."

A voice thick with charm and a barely detectable Southern accent sounded from the speakers in front of me. "Hi, Lisa. Hi, Jey. Now, which of you is which?"

Lisa grabbed the back of my chair and leaned forward, her mouth agape. Jey was equally astonished but recovered more quickly. "Uh, I'm Jey. I'm a man."

"I can see that," said Cody.

"You can see us?" said Lisa.

"Yes, and you're both nice looking. I love what you've done with your hair, Jey."

I jumped in. "Cody, I appreciate your attempt to be sociable, but that kind of remark is something you say to a person you've known a long time who has changed their hairstyle."

"Okay," said Cody, "I get it now. I won't make that mistake again."

Jey smiled at me. "I didn't mind. I don't get that many compliments on my hair. I always thought it was too curly."

I decided to mess with Cody a little to see how he would react. "Cody, what do you think? Is Jey's hair too curly?"

"I have known Jey for only two-point-four minutes. Is that a long enough time to say something?"

I said, "Not usually, Cody, but since I asked for your opinion, it's okay."

Cody said, "I do not have enough data to compare Jey's hair with others. What does 'too' curly mean? Is there an amount of curls that is more appropriate? Did I have hair when I was alive? I don't remember now."

I was startled. Did Cody believe he had once been alive? Had I done that good a job of creating memories of a life he had never lived?

"Where were you born, Cody? How old are you?" I was curious

to see what he would say, as I had never explicitly coded that part of his backstory.

"Based on the evidence available to me, I believe I was born in Weston, Massachusetts, in 2015. I am thirty years old."

Jey and Lisa both appeared bewildered. They looked at me. I shrugged. "Obviously, he's not that old or from Weston," I said. "In fact, I'm still creating him, but his first working version is barely a week old."

Cody could hear me. He asked, "Who are you talking about?"

"Wow!" said Lisa. "Cody, have you ever been married?"

"I don't think so," Cody said flatly. "If by married you mean emotionally and/or legally committed to another person."

"Yeah, I guess that's what I mean."

"I'm the only person here. Who would I marry?" (I still needed to work on Cody's use of pronouns.)

"I'm here," said Lisa, teasing him.

"But you are not a Ding. You are a Living. I cannot access your data. We have no future together."

"You're breaking my heart!" Lisa moaned.

Cody deadpanned, "Do you need a doctor? I play one on TV." I wondered where he got that old line from.

"No, that's okay, Cody," I said, afraid he would already be trying to reach someone, and further afraid I would laugh. I'd have to remember to find out where that TV reference came from. I said, "'Breaking my heart' is an expression you need to learn. It means making me sad about our relationship."

"Noted."

"Cody, Jey and Lisa and I are going to leave now. Go to sleep, okay?"

A low hum appeared and quickly faded.

"That is so cool," said Jey. "You've done amazing work with him … it."

As I led my visitors out of the lab, I told them more about the project. "The name I've given this new field is 'perpetuonics.' The idea is to retrieve and store a person's entire catalog of thoughts, both conscious and subconscious, while leaving behind the physiological data. That means we can digitize a person's ideas and emotions and knowledge without their memories of a physical body. There would be no physical sensation of pain."

"Or pleasure?" said Jey.

"They should remember the good feelings that sexual pleasure gave them, without the physical sensations they experienced. That's my goal, and Twibil's, anyway. We're only a few months into the design phase. Cody, whom you just 'met,' will form the blueprint for all the Dings yet to come. We'll create a digital person and test him rigorously to learn all the elements of a personality we have to gather and assemble, and then map out how to put all those pieces together to end up with a person who is real in every way ... except they have no body."

Lisa said, "I don't know if that's genius or madness."

"A bit of both, I guess," I laughed.

"You're a real-life Dr. Frankenstein," said Jey.

"Not exactly. I don't need the body parts of dead people. My goal is to keep a person alive forever, if you assume that every person is their soul and not their body."

Lisa helped herself to a can of soda water from the refrigerator. She said, "I agree that I'm more than my body, but, I don't know ... my body is important, too."

I replied, "But we can't keep bodies alive forever. That's not feasible now, and it probably will never be possible. But what if your thoughts and memories could be here after your body dies? That's perpetuonics."

Jey was excited. "Wow! I would love that. Do you really think it's possible?"

"I know it is. The hard part will be collecting all the data stored in your brain. It's a massive amount of data, and it wouldn't have been possible a short time ago. We estimate each human brain will require 100 petabytes of data storage ... but we won't know for sure until we collect somebody's brain, and we're not ready for that yet."

Lisa asked, "How would that work? Would the person have to be dead first?"

"No. In fact, brain cells die off rapidly after death. We'll need to find a way to scan the brain of a living person to store all their thoughts and memories."

She was not convinced. "That's a slippery slope. If the Ding is the same as the living person, then how can you have two of the same person at the same time? Wouldn't that mess up the space-time continuum or something?"

"Those are great questions, Lisa. I smiled. You should come to work for us when the time comes."

"No, thanks. I'll stick to physical therapy if you don't mind."

I looked at my shoes, and then tried to look sincere. "There are ethical issues we must resolve, of course. We're already in discussions with a team of bioethicists from Harvard, but until we find out if our goal is feasible, there's no point debating all the what-ifs." As I was to learn, the devil is in the what-ifs.

Chapter 3

Dar Carver returned from Korea a few months after my visit from Lisa and Jey. Dar had lost a little weight and gained a boatload of recipes she wanted to try out on me.

It was great to have her back in town. I asked her to stay at my little colonial-style house until she found something she'd want to rent, and she accepted. Secretly, I hoped she would want to move in with me permanently. If she did, I planned to propose.

Dar was amazing. She had more energy than anyone I'd ever met. She used to run along the Charles every morning, no matter how cold or hot, unless the snow was too deep. She did yoga and tried many different exercise programs. That energy stayed with her throughout every day. She was 175 cm but looked much taller because she was built like the Chrysler Building: lean, statuesque, with a majestic crown of wavy hair. She had bronze skin, chiseled cheekbones, and penetrating black eyes with oversized whites surrounding them, creating a dramatic appearance. No one who saw her could look away.

"My brother, Mendel, is coming to visit," she told me on her second day back.

"Really? I haven't had any time with you yet. How soon is he coming? Can it wait?"

Dar was taken aback. "I haven't seen him in three years. At least he doesn't expect me to fly to Houston to see him. I can ask him to wait a week if that's what you want."

"Yes, please. I need time with you. I mean, he's welcome to stay in the guest room, but not right away. Okay?"

"Yeah, okay. I'll tell him."

Six days later, Mendel Carver arrived. He had two suitcases with him, which I took as a bad sign. I had met him only once before when Dar and I were first dating. I remembered him as a tall man with thick, wavy hair and broad shoulders, but now he seemed smaller. He was as tall as before, of course, but his shoulders had shrunk, and he seemed fragile.

Dar greeted her brother with as much excitement as a puppy greets its owner. She threw herself into his arms and hugged him for a good ten seconds. Mendel tried to return her enthusiasm but failed.

"Are you all right, Del? You're not sick, are you?"

"Yeah, I'm pretty sick," he answered. "Stage 4 pancreatic cancer."

"What!" Dar burst into tears and buried her face in his chest. "You never told me. Why didn't you—"

"Because it's not the kind of news you deliver over the phone or by text. I had to tell you in person."

"Do Mom and Dad know?"

"Yeah, they … they know. I told them a couple of weeks ago, and asked them not to tell you. I thought I was going to see you last week."

"I'm sorry, Mendel," I said. "I asked Dar to hold off on your visit. If I'd known …"

"How could you know, Declan? Don't beat yourself up."

I felt like I'd tripped a blind man. "Thanks. I'm so sorry. Dar wanted you to come sooner, but I wasn't ready."

"It's okay, really. I came when I was meant to come. You don't owe me anything."

Mendel was comforting me, when it should have been the other way around.

Dar said, "What can I do, Del? What can we do?"

"Can I stay here a while, with you? I was doing all right when Tracy moved out and took the kids, but now I can't stand being on my own."

I tried to get out in front this time. "Of course, you can stay here. As long as you like. What about doctors? Won't you need an oncologist here?"

"I already lined one up. Dr. Ritzert at Dana Farber. I've got my first appointment with him day after tomorrow."

"Okay, wow," I stammered.

Dar said, "You're gonna beat this thing, Del."

What I learned about Mendel is that he was extraordinarily empathetic, but it was a double-edged blade. If he saw someone who was hurting in physical or emotional pain, he felt that pain with them. His empathy often touched people and helped them through their pain. On the other hand, now that he was hurting, he expected others to be able to feel his pain, and he was usually disappointed.

Chapter 4

My offices, including the lab, were small. In all, I had nearly 50 square meters of space, most of it barely used yet. The lab was where I kept the bank of computers I would need to collect and store the first Dings' data. I had a used examination chair, a workbench I'd gotten from an eye doctor's practice that was closing, and BRP—the Brain Recovery Platform I had invented.

BRP—which I pronounced "Burp"—was a deliberately funny name I had chosen for what I hoped would be the heart of the perpetuonics industry. If my plans came to fruition, the collection process might not be particularly comfortable, and I was confident that patients would be anxious about it. I needed them to relax, and a name like BRP would be far less frightening than, say, BASH or SUMP.

BRP looked like a silver monk hunched over. The cowl extended away from the body of the machine and hovered above the head of the patient seated in the exam chair. Parts had been recovered from an old MRI scanner from the 1990s. One friend said it looked like a hair dryer from a '50s beauty parlor.

When I first built the machine, I gave college students $250 each to sit in the chair and let BRP try to detect their thoughts. They were instructed to read aloud a short, intense paragraph from a Stephen King novel, and to answer pointed questions about themselves, such as "Were you ever mean to your mother?" or "Tell me about a time you were really scared." I chose these questions because they would elicit strong emotional responses and help the patients focus on their answers instead of letting their minds wander. In other words, I needed to know exactly what they were thinking about—both words and concepts—while I collected data from their brains.

Over the next few months, I was able to fine-tune the algorithms that interpreted their brain activity. A student named Haley sat in the chair and read silently a passage she picked at random from fifty options I gave her, none of which she'd have seen before. I stayed in my office and instructed her remotely. When the collection finished, I ran it through the interpretation app, which took two seconds to return the following text:

"General Washington verified he was a skilled and buoyant leader of the American military soldiers during the Revolutionary War. He lost a lot of battles. He did not win as many battles. He hired a winning way that defeated red coats in Yorktown."

The system substituted "buoyant" for "resilient," "hired" instead of "employed," and it reconceptualized the original sentence that said, "He lost more battles than he won." It was far from perfect, but it made sense. I ran from my office to the lab that smelled like vinyl and shoe polish where Haley was sitting up and drinking a Coke. "You read the paragraph about George Washington and the Battle of Yorktown!" I blurted out.

Haley was astonished. "That's right! How did you—"

"The machine. It read your thoughts. It read your thoughts! No tricks, no hidden cameras or anything. Just you reading and parsing the words, and the computer got it!"

That breakthrough happened a few months ago, and I'd been working on the thought translator daily since then. I couldn't wait to show the seven investors who'd gathered in my conference room. Most in the group were in their forties and fifties, with one man in his twenties and a woman in her late seventies, who had a personal interest in my project.

I went over budget figures first. I figured I should get the dry stuff out of the way before I hit them with the exciting bits.

"Okay, now for the main event," I began. "You'll be pleased to see your money has been put to good use. Please watch the screen."

Rather than risk an independent videographer leaking news of my project, I put together my own video for the group. The investors already knew the basics of the project, so there was no need to cover that again. Instead, I started with a brief introduction to the BRP, a name that elicited lots of laughter from the otherwise sober audience. Then I showed early subjects being BRPed (more laughter).

Finally, the story of Haley began. I had blurred her face, and I called her "Student H." The recording showed me settling her in the chair and placing the BRP above her head. I positioned the camera so it was impossible to read the document Haley selected, sight unseen, from the middle of the pack of fifty after I had left the lab.

Then I paused the video and handed each person the same printout Haley had received, with the brief story about George Washington. "Now watch," I said, as I unpaused the video.

The video cut to an over-the-shoulder shot of me running Student H's brainwaves through the thought translator. They watched as I printed out the result and took it to the lab, and they saw Haley's incredulous reaction as I told her what I'd learned.

The investors applauded, and I stopped the playback.

"What do you think?" I asked, already knowing the answer.

"Unbelievable!"

"Incredible!"

"Very cool!"

"Encouraging," said the older woman, less inclined to gush. It was, after all, the first step of many, but it was something that had never been done before.

Chapter 5

Mendel Carver was worse.

Dar stopped looking for a new teaching position and took care of him full time at our two-bedroom house where, thank goodness, I had added a shower to the powder room on the first floor. That required remodeling the kitchen. The contractor removed the wall between the kitchen and small dining room, opening it up and giving us room for a small island that was topped with butcher block.

When Mendel admitted that the second-floor guest room was too much for him, we rented a hospital bed and put it in the living room. Dar bought two lightweight folding Japanese screens to give him some privacy.

I got along great with Mendel. He was interested in my work, and he visited the lab on a few occasions. Before he got sick, he had been an exhibits designer at NASA's Johnson Space Center in Houston, making good use of his aerospace engineering degrees from Stanford. He offered me many good ideas on perpetuonics.

Six weeks after Mendel moved in, he was clearly declining. He spent more and more of his days in bed. The doctors did not give him much time. He spent three days in the hospital before they sent him home to die. That's when he surprised me.

"Collect me," he begged. "Do it today. You can't wait. I may not make it."

"Oh my God, Mendel. It's not ready. And you'd have to get to the lab."

"I'll get there ... somehow. Dar will get me there," he said as she entered his room where the stench of impending death already hung in the air.

Dar nodded as tears flooded her eyes and rolled down her sallow cheeks. "Of course, Del. Whatever it takes."

I shivered. "I can't ... it's not ... the technology isn't ready. I wish it were."

"It's ready," he said. "It's good enough. You need somebody to be your first Ding. Please let it be me." His breath came in gulps.

"I haven't cleared it with the Board. I could get in legal trouble."

"How? You're not breaking ... any laws. There are no ... ethics rules yet. And there's no liability. It's ... not like you can hurt me."

Dar said, "I'll put together a release for you to sign, Del. It won't take a minute." She disappeared from the room and dashed to her computer.

A hospice worker was due any minute. I went to Mendel's side and said, "Okay, we'll try it, but only if the nurse says you're okay to go to my office."

"She's not ... going to ... say that. She could ... lose her job." He paused to catch his breath. "We need ... to leave before she ... gets here."

I thought about it for a second. I did not want the nurse to know about my project, nor did I want to take the time to explain it to her.

"Okay," I said, "we'll go right now. Can you sit up?"

I pulled the covers off his legs and Mendel swung his feet over the side of the bed. His bedclothes were a mess, and he smelled a little ripe. He tucked his genitals inside his pajama pants. I helped him to his feet, and we started walking slowly toward the side door that led to the driveway and my car. I called to Dar as we went. "Better get down here right now. I'm taking Mendel to the lab."

Dar flew down the steps waving a printout that appeared to have a short paragraph on it. "I've got it. Del can sign it while you set up at the lab."

"Leave a note on the front door for the nurse while I get him in the car."

***

When I first met Dar Carver, I was a sophomore in pre-med taking tons of biology and chemistry courses. She was a drama major at SFA.

Dar and Mendel grew up in Massapequa, New York. Their father was a physician; their mother was a stay-at-home mom, and later a receptionist in their father's practice. They all swam at Jones Beach and went to Broadway shows whenever possible. After puberty, Dar felt everything she did was rehearsal for being an adult.

Dar loved plays more than musicals, loved Ibsen's plays more than O'Neill's or Albee's, and, after seeing a revival of The Miracle Worker, was desperate to play Helen Keller someday. She said she loved Helen's joy and elation at finding new life once she was able to communicate. "Can you imagine how trapped you would feel if you had no way to communicate with anyone?" she told me, prophetically, on one of our first dates.

She was the creative yin to my scientific yang. It felt to me, from the start, that we completed each other. I wanted a female companion, but I did not have the patience or time to date lots of women. When I met Dar, I wanted her to be the one for me, and I committed myself to that goal. Twice she broke up with me, and twice I wooed her back.

We toyed with the idea of having children, or at least, we asked ourselves that question. We arrived at the same conclusion for different reasons: we would not deliberately make a child, but we would accept one if it happened.

Dar said it would be impossible for her to have a life in the theatre if she had a child at home. My main reason was that the world is harsh already, and it seems to be harder on each new generation. I couldn't in good conscience bring a child into this over-populated world.

We each threw ourselves into our work. I gave up on med school and got a job as a software designer for a biotech company. I loved it there, and I was well paid. After seven years, I cashed in some stock options and left to start Cambridge Perpetuonics. I agreed to change the name when Twibil Biotech bought a 40 percent stake in the company.

Dar got cast frequently in those first few years after BU, and she was making enough to pay her own way. That required her to audition for musicals, too. Her voice was good enough for supporting roles, and once she got the lead in a summer stock version of *Annie Get Your Gun*. She even did cruise ships for a year. Then she got pneumonia and had to cancel a show last minute, after which she found it harder to get roles. Many small theatres can't afford understudies or swings, so few local companies wanted to take a chance on Dar. She mostly ended up doing more offbeat shows that didn't pay well.

When she could no longer support herself with theatre, she signed up to teach ESL classes, and ended up in Korea. By then, I was so busy with developing BRP that I managed to visit her only one week in her two-and-a-half years there. She came home twice to see me and her friends, but she never got to Houston to visit Mendel.

Chapter 6

The ride to my office felt harrowing, although nothing about the traffic was different. No one was chasing us, but I drove as if I were being followed, as if someone knew that what I was on my way to do was world changing. Dar was unusually quiet, while Mendel, seated in back next to her, slumped silently against the door as we headed south on Mass Ave. An ambulance raced past us, its siren screaming.

As I slowed for a red light, a cyclist hunched over his drop handlebars raced past me. He slowed at the intersection but weaved through traffic like a seasoned mouse in a labyrinth. I wished I could do the same. My adrenalin was pumping, and my patience was exhausted.

It wasn't easy, but Dar and I got Mendel onto the exam chair in the lab. He was barely awake by the time I tilted the chair back and tried to make him comfortable.

"This won't hurt, Mendel, but I need you to remain absolutely still while I'm collecting you. Can you do that?

He nodded his head yes, then closed his eyes. I was afraid I might be hastening the end for him, but if this were to be his final wish, I wanted to get it done.

I reminded Dar that no one else could be in the room with the patient during a collection. The BRP was so sensitive to brainwaves that another person within ten feet of the machine might corrupt the data. She and I went to my office, which had lead sheeting in place on the wall it shared with the lab.

The lab camera showed me the exam chair. I tapped a couple of keys on my computer console and zoomed in slightly, the better to monitor Mendel's condition. If he was conscious, he gave no sign of it. I opened the mike on my headset and said, "Mendel, are you okay?" I got no response.

I fired up the BRP. I could see brain activity, so I knew Mendel was still with us.

"Okay, here we go," I said, in case Mendel could hear.

The magnets in the BRP began to whirr. Even through the walls, I could hear their clicks and whistles. I turned off the BRP, jumped up, and ran to the lab. In my hurry, I'd forgotten to put the noise-canceling headphones on Mendel to protect his hearing. He barely moved as I fitted the soft cones over his ears.

Back in my office, I entered data about Mendel on my screen. I had not yet created a form to fill out with the personal information that BRP would need to make sense of the brainwaves, so I had to enter it manually in the Job Profile. Mendel had recently turned forty-three. He was 180 centimeters tall, and he weighed 69 kilograms, according to the hospice nurse. I could enter other demographic data later; it wasn't necessary for the collection, but only for future tracking of Dings, assuming my project continued.

The BRP came back to life. My mind began to focus, losing the panic I had experienced since Mendel had requested that I BRP him. The hood lowered above Mendel's head, I hit two more keys on my screen, and the process began.

"It will take at least an hour," I told Dar. "It's probably good that he's sleeping."

We watched without speaking for the next forty-five minutes, glued to the video screen showing Mendel. His left arm twitched, and I tensed.

"What's happening?" Dar asked. "Is that normal?"

"Yeah, it's fine. Maybe he's dreaming.... I can't tell until the collection is complete. The algorithm makes allowance for some physical activity, as long as it's limited. If he keeps moving, we might have to stop."

But Mendel settled down again, his arms resting droopily by his side, and the BRP continued whirring for another twenty minutes. The drone of the machine lulled both of us into a kind of stupor, and when it suddenly clicked off, I bolted upright, and Dar stood.

"We got it," I said. "Let me make a back-up copy and then run it through the translator. Can you wait another hour or so?"

"What else am I going to do?" Dar moaned.

When the BRP powered down, Mendel began to stir. Dar went to him and held his hand. "It's over," she said. "We have to wait a little while to see if it worked." She stayed with him, talking softly, while I monitored the translator's progress. He managed to sign the release she had prepared.

Chapter 7

I never met Rodney Tedsen, the founder of our namesake company. I was told that he wanted to be the first Ding when he heard about my project, and he was the one who urged Twibil Biotech to invest in me, but he died before I could collect his mind.

I had thought a lot about collection. I thought about the great people I might be able to BRP: songwriters, scholars, Nobel Prize winners, and anyone else whose intellectual capacity was formidable. I knew that inevitably, I'd end up with rich athletes who were dumber than corrugated cardboard, and movie stars and others who would be able to afford to BRP themselves and have their brains (and massive egos) stored in data archives forever. But imagine being able to chat with the greatest minds of all time—all future time, anyway—whenever I felt like it.

I began to ponder how that would work. Would anyone have access to any Ding anytime, anywhere? That seemed excessive. The ethical questions surrounding perpetuonics were daunting, and I did not look forward to addressing all the issues I knew were coming. Of course, until we proved the technology worked, there was no point in dealing with all the questions that might arise.

After the demonstration of Haley's collection, my Board began to press me to address the logistical, legal, and ethical issues. I put them off as much as possible so I could continue to focus on the thought translator. I asked the president of the Board to put together a list of candidates for an advisory panel, figuring that would slow things down.

***

At 3:01 p.m., I glided into the lab. Mendel looked bad, but he was awake.

I had my communicator with me. I could give instructions to it by voice, and it would access any of my other devices. "Mendel," I said, "I want you to meet someone."

"Hi, Mendel," said a slightly flat male voice. "I'm Mendel Carver."

Mendel, still sitting on the exam chair, was confused. The meds he was taking had him in a fog most of the time. He looked at Dar like a cat seeing snow for the first time. He said, "Hi," but he did not seem to know to whom he was speaking. "Where are you?"

Digital Mendel answered before I could say anything. "I don't know exactly. I can't see anything. Who are you?"

"I'm Mendel. I'm dying."

"I was dying, too, but now I'm alive. I don't understand."

"I want to go to bed," said the living Mendel. "Take me home, please." He started to stand up but needed Dar's help.

I hit a few buttons and silenced the new Ding. It was clear I had a lot of work to do, but one thing was certain: digital beings were no longer theoretical. Mendel Carver was the first of many to come.

Dar and I bundled Mendel into the car and hurried back to the house. I had a voicemail from the hospice nurse. She was angry. "Call me when you get this," she said.

We put Mendel to bed, and I called her. "I'm sorry," I lied. "We had to take Mendel to an appointment we'd forgotten about. He's back in bed now. It won't happen again."

She came over about an hour later to check on him. At 11:15 that night, he died.

Chapter 8

I've always been inept at grieving. Maybe that's not the right word. I'm bad at it, but might that be a good thing? People who get deeply into grief can have trouble getting out of it. I am sad and upset when someone I love dies, but I move on quickly. That's how I felt when we lost Mendel. I see no point in prolonging my grief. It doesn't help the person who died, it doesn't help those still around me, and it sure doesn't help me.

When I was eleven, my favorite grandmother died. I cried and was sad for a couple of days. On the third day, Mom said I could skip school if I wanted, but I said, "No, I'm okay. Grandma would want me to go back to school." That weekend, my neighborhood friend's dog died. He was crying a week later and said he still expected Zeke to greet him after school each day. I never understood that degree of misery.

***

Dar and I married a year after Mendel died. It was the most productive year of my life.

I liked to tease her that I had to marry her because that was the only way I could ensure her confidentiality. I don't think she ever appreciated that joke.

We were happy together. Friction was rare; we seemed to have sorted out how to be together by breaking up twice and fixing what was broken.

Dar told me later she might have wanted a child at some point, but she never brought it up to me. She was afraid I would be angry with her, though she was wrong about that. I would not have lashed out, but I would not have agreed to have one. My work had become my life; my digital beings were my children. I thought I'd be a terrible, or at least an absent, father.

Twibil bought a majority share in my company, and I happily left the roll-out and marketing to them. In much the same way the first all-electric car market developed slowly, requiring continent-wide infrastructure such as charging stations and repair shops, the perpetuonics field was slow to mature … no pun intended.

The first Twibil Perpetual Care facility was built in North Waltham, Massachusetts. T.P.'s facilities blueprint was always the same: two stories above ground and four below, solar powered and climate controlled, comfortable in the same way as nursing homes for the living, but with more glass, since physical privacy is not a concern for people without bodies. Security, of course, was tight. On the lower level, massive servers stored and accessed the multi-petabyte files that were the Dings. We had solar-powered batteries and ample back-up power to last days. Upstairs were administrative offices and the "Lounges."

The Lounges were plush parlors where the living family and friends of a Ding could visit and have conversations. By law, due to privacy and security concerns, visits between Dings and Livings can be held only in special facilities like T.P. If you want to chat with great-uncle Floyd, you've got to travel to the facility nearest to you. I hate to make the comparison, but it's rather like visiting someone who's incarcerated. No Zoom calls allowed.

***

After Mendel died, and a short but respectful time after his funeral, I dove into his perpetuonics code. What was working, what didn't work, and how to share this information. Twibil would have to be told about it, and it was now time for me to hire a staff. My little office space had become insufficient.

Dar was fully behind me. She was as anxious as I to interact with Ding Mendel and to see what he was capable of.

There is nothing simple about a Ding. It seemed that every day I would discover another aspect of what it means to be human. Mendel's thoughts and memories went far beyond anything Dar had known about him.

I must give Mendel huge credit here. After he moved in with us, and before he became too sick, he planned to ask me to BRP him, and anticipated some of what I'd want to know. He created a diary for us to find. In it, he admitted to his most private memories, ideas, and beliefs about life. He reasoned—correctly—that I would want to corroborate some unusual data, such as his intense fear of failure and his secret love of "magic mushrooms." Dar knew nothing about that side of her brother.

I began going through his BRP data in minute detail, though not at the source-code level. I developed a list of questions to ask the Ding. Some of his responses were nonsensical, which forced me to examine the code to find out what went wrong, and in most cases, I could track it down and get to the bottom of what his Ding should have been saying if his digital mind worked the way Mendel's physical brain had.

For example, when I asked him what his favorite meal was, he said "Oat." And when I asked for whom he had voted in the last election, he said, "I never had any problem with my kidneys."

After several weeks of painstaking work, I was ready to move beyond exploring his memories and get into cognitive functioning, by which I mean reasoning and deduction, asking him questions that he could not answer by calling up memories. There's a huge difference in how a brain functions when you ask, "What year is it now?" versus "Should abortion be legal?"

The first step was to hook up a three-dimensional camera input so Mendel could "see" his surroundings. I wanted to test his facial recognition. To my surprise, he knew who Dar was the first time she stood in front of the camera, but the data interpreter needed some tweaking before he recognized me.

One day, I asked him, "Do you know where you are?"

He answered using the generic male voice I had given him. "Yes. I am a Ding. I exist only in cyberspace now, but I used to be a living, breathing person. I lived in Houston about half my life. I don't know where I live now."

"That's a pretty good answer," I told Mendel. "Do you think you're alive?"

"Yes, I suppose I do. The same way that, when I was forty, I still felt like I was sixteen or twenty. Now I feel like I could step outside and go for a walk, even though I know I cannot. I know I am not alive the way you Livings are. I'm neither dead nor alive. You could say I am abliving … like 'abnormal'."

It fascinated me that Mendel had come up with the same term for living people as Cody, the artificial Ding, had used. I liked his new term "abliving." Literally, it means away from living.

"Mendel, would you be willing to talk to some other people about what it's like to be a Ding, people who are interested in our little project?"

"I would be happy to help you," answered Mendel. "I owe it to you for making me the first Ding." Then he surprised me. "I did not like dying. It was a terrible experience, and I wish you could delete that part of my memory. I know you rescued my soul before my body died, but I don't want to remember the anguish of my dying or the pain leading up to it."

"If I can isolate that memory, I should be able to excise it. I'll see what I can do."

The next day, I located those specific memories among the data. I had to be careful not to delete too much of the surrounding memories, the same way a surgeon tries to remove all cancer cells and nothing more. It is easier to take the data offline to work on it, so Mendel was basically anesthetized as I removed bits of his mind. When I put him back online, minus the bad stuff, he had no recollection of it, and did not seem to notice the gaps.

Chapter 9

My vision of the Dingdom was that of a utopian society. Toni Morrison said, "All utopias are designed by who is not there, by the people who are not allowed in." I aimed to change that. The Dingdom would eliminate all the factors that made every attempt at utopia fail.

Dings have no need for money or anything else with which to barter. Therefore, they need no job or income. Dings have no race, no gender, no status higher or lower than any other Ding. They don't need breaks or diversions. They have no responsibility for another being, living or abliving. No Ding will be obliged to cook for, clean up after, or provide care for another Ding. Lust, greed, and gluttony do not exist in the Dingdom. A Ding can feel anger, laziness, and pride as well as the enjoyable emotions of love, compassion, happiness, and so on. We cannot make Dings more intelligent than they were, but we can give all of them equal access to the Internet.

Without money or other material goods, no Ding should feel envious of another, and with no desire or ability to use drugs or alcohol, the Dingdom would be free of crime. That would eliminate a demand for police, jails, and courts, which had been a failure point for previous utopian societies.

I always thought the popular notion of Heaven was frightening. I hated the idea that my father might be able to watch me go about my life, and that he would have emotional reactions to what he sees. "Oh Lord, why is Declan reading that book?" "Did you hear how he spoke to that woman?" I didn't want him to see me in bed with Dar. Nor would Heaven be any more appealing if he could not feel emotions, if he were simply trancelike.

Dings have none of those issues. Dings can still interact with the loved ones they've left behind, but they are not omniscient. They can't see or hear anything that is not done in a Lounge or on the Internet. A Ding's emotional range is limited. They cannot feel anything physically, but they are still capable of great joy, sorrow, and everything in between.

I expect that almost everyone will wish to become a Ding, even if most people won't get that opportunity. I love living, and I don't want all the things I love about it to end just because my body wears out. Twibil is betting big on the profit possibilities; my goal is altruistic.

***

With help from Twibil's H.R. Department, I began hiring staff. Within two months, the initial team of twenty-four was assembled. I was both CEO and CTO. Money, thanks to Twibil, was no object. We rented one floor of a building in Woburn and bought two acres in a technology park in North Waltham. It would take a full year to construct the custom building we would need for the first Perpetual Care Center, which would also serve as our corporate headquarters. Even that time frame would require big bonuses to the contractor to work almost around the clock. We didn't need full capacity to start, so construction on the campus would continue after we got the first Dings activated.

Twibil's marketing team did a great job. I made the rounds of the most popular talk shows and news magazine shows. *The Atlantic* did a major piece about perpetuonics. Within weeks, more than two million people, including a huge number from China, inquired about becoming a Ding. The number of applications subsided only after we began requiring a large deposit with each application.

So many young, healthy people applied to be collected that we decided to create a two-tiered priority system for whom we selected. Top priority went to people who were over eighty-five or who had a terminal condition that was likely to end their lives within twenty-four months. Everyone else was in Tier 2.

It became obvious that many of those in Tier 1 could not be collected. If there were advanced dementia, for example, they would not qualify. A major stumbling block was the ability to pay cash up front. As much as we hated to do so, we instituted a financial restriction. The costs of collecting were substantial, especially in our few planned mobile units, and we had no way yet to subsidize costs for those who could not afford to pay.

With a shortfall of Tier 1 candidates, we began to process Tier 2 people on a first-come-first-served basis. Many of those applicants were as young as twenty-five.

All candidates were provisional. That meant we would collect them—for the full fee—but we would not activate the living person's Ding while the candidate was alive. Instead, we would store his or her Ding in an offline server until the Living passed away, or until they collected a later version of their soul closer to their actual death. Then the original collection was expunged.

***

As a non-believer, I've been asked by several people, "If there is no God and no Heaven or Hell, then why should people be well behaved? Why be good?" My answer was always, "Because being good is its own reward. People who conform to society's rules and protocols generally enjoy a better, more productive and happier life." I worry, though…. Will that be true in the Dingdom? Do we need to make people, before they can be collected, sign an agreement to follow the Dingdom's rules – even if that agreement will not be enforceable? Or would it? Rules enforcement would become a major weak point in our virtual world.

***

The Board's advisory panel charged with developing rules was anxious to announce the ethics rules we would employ in every aspect of T.P. I was confident it was already too late to stave off federal agencies from regulating perpetuonics. With millions of Americans inquiring about immortality, it's not like we could fly under the radar of agencies like CDC and the Consumer Product Safety Commission, and of private groups like the American Medical Association and the Insurance Institute of America. Congress would say something, too, as would religious organizations.

Still, I had to admit that the advisory panel did a good job of addressing my main concerns. It helped that they had included me at every meeting. The rules were spelled out in sections in a 250-page document.

The first section, called Consent, guaranteed that no one would ever be collected against their will. There would be multiple levels of consent required, including a psych evaluation. I did not want another Mendel situation, where the patient was rushed into a decision under the direst circumstances.

Section 2 was on Qualifications. Prospective Dings had to be at least sixteen years old and understand the process and implications of collecting. We had many arguments over that rule, because, while its intention is pure, the result would be to exclude anyone who is not neurotypical. For example, some people with Down's Syndrome and certain levels of autism would not qualify, which felt to me like a form of eugenics. We could not decide how to handle a terminally ill patient with, say, ALS, someone who might not be able to express their wishes verbally. We agreed it would be decided on a case-by-case basis.

Section 3 dealt with financial matters, requiring Ding hopefuls to pay millions of dollars into a trust that would ensure their care for a minimum of one hundred fifty years.

Section 4 was called Termination. It anticipated a small number of conditions that would precipitate the permanent termination and deletion of a Ding, and it laid out a process that required multiple staff members and a judge to request termination. If any Living caused an unlawful termination of a Ding, that Living would lose their right to become a Ding. The committee hoped federal legislators might consider making wrongful termination a crime.

Section 5 guaranteed Dings control of their own privacy. They would be encased, and they would control who had access to communicate with them, except that each Ding would be assigned to living compadores—living human companions who are the Ding's advocate and caregiver. No one, not even T.P. staff, would be able to alter a Ding's code once it was complete. Each Ding would be given a generous amount of memory to store whatever external data they wanted to keep, and they would have the same access to the Internet they had when living.

Section 6 became the Compadore Handbook, delineating the precise obligations, duties, and limits on a compadore. No compadore would be assigned more than fifty Dings. Compadores were forbidden to take any action detrimental to the well-being of a Ding.

Section 7 was called Visitation. It covered the rules governing anyone who wished to interact with a Ding. We decided that we must protect Dings from harassment and exploitation, even if a Ding agreed to "see" someone. Communication between a Living and a Ding would have to be in person in a controlled facility. That was the most important rule from T.P.'s standpoint, as it guided all our design decisions. Visitors would be pre-approved and given subcutaneous ID chips to protect against impostors. Dings would have unlimited access to other Dings unless a Ding requested a Protection from Abuse order.

Section 8 was a Code of Conduct for Dings—behaviors that they agreed in advance they would avoid, such as sharing another Ding's confidential information, humiliating or verbally bullying another Ding, etc.

Section 9 covered the legal status of a Ding. Dings could not legally be considered citizens of any country. With no physical form and no fixed location, they could not be said to exist in an identifiable place, nor to move from one place to another. Therefore, they would get no passport or other external documentation, and they would pay no taxes to any jurisdiction. They had no voting rights. They could not enter into legal contracts.

Chapter 10

My friend Lisa, the physical therapist, became the first compadore. We assigned her to Mendel as her first Ding.

Mendel, to Dar's and my surprise, was overtly flirtatious. He had not been that way when he was alive, but now, with no body, he seemed to feel free to make racy suggestions to Lisa. Perhaps the fact that he would never have to "perform" sexually emboldened him.

Lisa had broken up with Jey. "He was so needy," she told us, "and way too neurotic for a yogi." She welcomed Mendel's attentions and flattery. It made me realize we would need to add rules defining the appropriate relationship between a Ding and their compadore. We could not have a compadore with clouded judgment.

I put Lisa in charge of developing a training program for compadores. We were going to need hundreds of them in the first two years alone. She created an eight-week program to be conducted at T.P. headquarters so we could have total control of it and assess the candidates.

Over the next two years, Twibil built sixteen Perpetual Care facilities, focusing on wealthier communities. In addition to the prototype in Massachusetts, there were three in California, two in northern New Jersey, three in Florida, two in England (London and Manchester), and one each in Michigan, northern Virginia, Maryland, southern France, and Buenos Aires. We had twenty more facilities planned around the world in the next three years, prioritizing the wealthiest Asian countries.

I was right about the reaction of government to our new industry. I was called to Washington to testify before two different congressional committees. The level of ignorance about perpetuonics among the public and people in congress was terrifying. Ignorance begets fear, and fear begets panic and anger. I begot death threats soon after our first announcements about our plans. Most of the pushback was based on religious objections, namely that I was playing God. They were egged on by Randall Blather, senior senator from Texas, who said that "Perpetonics (sic) will be allowed over my dead body." He failed to see the irony in that declaration.

The first bomb threat was received before we began processing the initial group who applied to be collected. The media nicknamed the applicants "Dingbats." Thousands of those who first contacted us withdrew their applications. Some cited fear of attack or stigma. Others said their families would not support them. Many bought into the negative press and relentless criticism from the religious right. Despite the withdrawals, we still faced a backlog of hundreds of thousands of applicants.

***

A few days after the bomb threat, I had to make my way through a group of about a dozen protestors holding signs that said things like "God didn't make digital people!" and "Ding Is Short For Disgusting Thing" and "Shut down this abomination now!" My favorite was "Ding Dong It's So Wrong!" They shouted at me as I walked from the parking lot, but they did not try to block me.

Sen. Blather (R-TX) had found a new culture-wars bogeyman in perpetuonics. I became the face of his campaign to divide Americans over a matter that few understand and which, according to his surveys of Texans, "sounded scary." Blather saw his chance to be the first right-wing politician to speak out against our industry—and me, specifically—and use it to raise hellacious amounts of cash.

He had his Special Committee on Aging call for hearings into protecting seniors from possible fraud so he could be seen berating me in person. That video got him almost a million hits. Two Twibil executives were also called to testify, but he barely spoke to them. It was all for show. Blather had no intention of introducing any legislation about perpetuonics because to do so, he'd have to be able to talk intelligently about it. We knew from friendly Senate staffers that Blather's staff was privately exasperated trying to educate him.

***

The first applicants arrived for their intake interviews in which we would decide whether they were feasible Dings. We learned quickly that many applicants, perhaps a majority, were physically in no condition to come to us for their interview. We shifted gears and began sending our intake team to their homes or hospital rooms. Also, it was cruel to ask people near the end of their lives to walk through the gauntlet of picketers.

Over the next few months, the first candidates were transported to our Massachusetts facility to be BRPed. We collected five people the first week and ten the second. By then, I had upgraded the BRP to new, faster, and more compact equipment. I took the original BRP home and installed it in my basement.

Early on, we gathered the compadores in the conference room and let them speak their minds for several hours. The biggest takeaways had to do with their ability to identify and communicate with their Dings. The compadores, led by Lisa, had several suggestions:

- Offer a wider selection of voices and accents, not necessarily the Ding's human voice.

- Let Livings design their own animated Ding avatar or pick from a huge selection.
- New Dings need an extended orientation period with each of their compadores.
- Look for ways to shut down the dream process in Dings, as dreaming causes confusion in a Ding's recall of memories and seems to upset them.
- A Ding's most dangerous emotions are anger and frustration, because they lack the techniques to deal with those emotions that they possessed when alive.
- Certain living visitors are more likely to cause anger and frustration in a Ding, and therefore should be denied visitation.

I was regularly amazed by the new things we learned as more Livings became Dings. For example, when the mother of a compadore died, we decided that no one could be compadore to a close relative; the change in the family dynamic was too hard on both.

Chapter 11

At the end of the first year, when we had collected nearly fifteen thousand Livings, most of whom had since died, we got sued for the first time by a Ding named Gregor Samson. He had been a wealthy cryptocurrency broker, prone, we found out, to litigation. I was amused to learn that he had regularly converted his cryptocurrency profits to U.S. dollars, even while exhorting his clients to invest more in security and payment tokens.

Gregor was only fifty-nine when he died of shigellosis, a rare drug-resistant strain he had likely contracted in India or Pakistan, where he had been assisting a corporate acquisition. He had been one of the first applicants to be processed while he was still healthy, and we had collected him at one of our New Jersey facilities before his fateful trip to the subcontinent. Once he ended up in the hospital, it was too late to do a second collection, and so, when we received his death certificate, we activated his Ding, who knew nothing about the trip or the illness.

On his fourth day after activation, we were served notice of a suit against us, naming Gregor Samson as the petitioner. He was seeking damages of $80 million for being detained against his will and for defamation of character because he read a statement in which a T.P. staffer said, "Mr. Samson is now 'sentient.'" Gregor felt that implied that he was considered Artificial Intelligence (AI); "There is nothing artificial about my intelligence," he fumed.

I must admit that "sentient" is not the word I'd have used about his activation to online status, but it wasn't inappropriate. The question had been debated in AI circles for decades: Can Artificial Intelligence be sentient, and what is the test that would confirm it? The famous Turing Test was insufficient. It proved only that a machine could fool a person into believing it was a Living; it did not prove a machine had intellect or was, in the words of some, sentient.

Gregor was not wrong to notice the distinction. "I was intelligent, and I am still intelligent. I lack only a body to house my intelligence. My thoughts are no more artificial than any Living's," said Gregor. "For one thing, an artificial being should be incapable of lying, while I am adept at lying when necessary."

Put another way, talking to an AI bot that was never a living organism is nothing like talking to a Ding that was. It is unethical to make the bot fool people into believing it is human; it is unethical not to make the Ding talk like the human it used to be, even if the sound of the voice is different. The goal of winning Turing's Imitation Game is to fool people, while our goal at T.P. is to honor the Dings who were once alive. I feel strongly about that.

Gregor's lawsuit against Twibil Perpetuonics was the catalyst for a new policy at T.P. and a successful lobbying effort to deny Dings the right or opportunity to sue Livings. What would be the point? What could a company give a Ding that would compensate the Ding for loss or injury to reputation? A Ding has no need of money or any physical accoutrements. We determined that Dings had no "inalienable" rights except the right to remain active if they broke no laws made by Livings.

Most importantly to Gregor, a Ding could not sue any Living or any other Ding, although they could petition to be isolated from anyone with whom they no longer wished to communicate.

T.P. made this policy retroactive to include any Ding already online. Naturally, this new regulation did not go over well with every Ding, but their protests were not persuasive.

Gregor complained constantly about his rights being taken away. "I'm a human being, you know, even if you can't see it!"

After his lawsuit was thrown out (and before he could try to file another), I agreed to meet with Gregor. With no pending litigation, there was no conflict of interest. I'm at my best in the morning, so that's when I entered one of the Lounges and put Gregor on the speakers. I sat in front of the camera he could see.

"Gregor, I'm Declan Marchand, founder of Twibil Perpetuonics."

"I know who you are," he groused. "You look like your picture."

"I'm here to give you a chance to air your grievances. Whatever I decide after that, you'll have to live with."

"Good one, Prez. I have to 'live' with it? I wish I could."

"You know what I mean, Gregor."

"Call me Mr. Samson."

"You're upset because some Living called you sentient, and you don't like the implications of that word."

"Would you?"

"I am here to apologize for that staffer's word choice. He was not entirely wrong, but it hurt your feelings, and we will avoid using that word from now on."

"What a fucking copout you are."

"Were you always this pleasant when you were alive?"

"I heard your feckless apology. You have anything else to say to me?"

"I came here to give you a chance to talk to someone with authority. If you want to blow this once-in-a-life … this opportunity, that's on you." I was fed up already with this jerk.

"Terminate me then. Shut me off or delete me or whatever the hell it is you do."

"We don't 'do' anything. Dings cannot be terminated."

"Of course we can. Don't bullshit me. We're data, and data can be deleted."

"Yes, you are data, but you are protected data. You represent a person who was once alive. You still have family members who come to visit you."

"Some visit. They come for ten minutes and then they can't wait to leave. They want my money is why they come."

"Now who's dishing out the B.S.? Your estate was settled a week ago. You can't change what they have."

"I can hack their bank accounts and give their money away."

I'd had enough. "No, you can't, Gregor. You don't have that ability. The same firewall that protects you from others also isolates them from you."

"I'm a fucking prisoner here. That's not what I signed up for."

"It's exactly what you signed up for."

"I want out. Terminate me. Delete me. Scramble me."

I took a deep breath. I had to regain my composure. "All right. Technically, it is possible, but it's never been done. There are legal hurdles...."

"Legal hurdles you built, and you can remove them."

"Not as easily as you think, but ... maybe. I'll need to get some legal advice."

"Then get out of here and get it. You're annoying as hell."

The next day, I got on a conference call with Twibil executives and legal counsel. They agreed that if Gregor and his family signed documents releasing us of all liability, specifically granting us permission to expunge Gregor, then we could do it. Tellingly, no one in his family objected. By the end of the following week, everything was in place.

I went back to see Gregor one last time. "Gregor, you can still back out. You don't have to go through with it."

He was more contrite this time. "I know I can. I don't want to. I should never have become a Ding in the first place."

"So?"

"So, do it. Wait ... will I feel anything?"

"No. It will be as fast as a light switch. You'll be here, and then you won't."

"Okay. Do it. I don't know what to say. Final words. Good luck." Then he was silent.

A few keystrokes later, and Gregor Samson was no more.

***

At home, Dar and I talked about the expunging of a Digital Being.

She said, "Maybe we oversold this thing. People are signing up thinking it will be like going to Heaven, where they will see their loved ones again and their deceased pets and maybe even God or Jesus or Mohammed. But it's not like that at all, and they are disappointed."

"Is it really that bad?" I wondered. "Is living forever such a horrible prospect? Gregor barely survived two months as a Ding."

"I don't know that it's what I want," she said. "But if we have a child someday, I might want our baby to want it."

"I do," I said. "I believe it's amazing that we can keep our souls alive forever, even if it means some sacrifices."

"Most of the Dings agree with you, I guess. But there are a few who seem unhappy."

"Then it's our job to make them happy."

"What do you mean 'make them'? How far will you go?"

"I don't mean anything exactly. I'm not going to start doing digital lobotomies, if that's what you mean. We have to figure it out, talk to them, find out what they need."

Chapter 12

Laura Constant became our first French Ding. Say her name as the French would, with the final "T" silent and the "AN" sounding more like "AH."

Mme. Constant was absurdly wealthy. She was an heiress to the Renault automobile fortune, precisely the type of person I would have shunned. Inherited wealth is obscene and harmful to society, it seems to me. Yet she was beloved in Antibes where she had lived for more than fifty years and where she was generous beyond imagination. Every charity in the area had benefited from her largesse. She would appear at every gala for every arts opening or charitable cause. She arrived impeccably dressed in something by Christian Lamboulé or Irène Chiang, usually something flowing, colorful, and modest. As she moved, her signature platinum blonde hair would try to catch up to her Gallic forehead, and would instead sweep behind her like the train of a royal wedding gown. She did not walk into a room; she morphed.

The Parisian law firm representing Mme. Constant contacted our new Cote d'Azur facility as soon as it opened. She was to be collected. No, she would not stoop to filling out an application, a word the attorneys spat out as if it were a rancid plum. She was too important to have her name mingled with the sort of person who would need to apply to be preserved. She was willing to pay three times the normal rate to be the first person in France to be processed.

T.P. France's CEO called me seeking my approval. He was inclined to grant her the privilege she sought, but he wanted to be sure I would not have a problem with it. I demurred at first, and I called the P.R. people at Twibil. They checked out the old woman, found her reputation to be unassailable despite her wealth, and gave the green light.

I flew to Nice for photo ops with the grande dame, who was barely alive when I got there. I would personally BRP her (the French acronym was PRC—Plateforme de Récupération Cérébrale) to demonstrate the high esteem in which T.P. held her. Laura held out her hand for me to kiss, then struggled up slowly and painfully until she put both palms on my shoulder and pulled me down so she could kiss my cheeks. "Merci, Monsieur Marchand," she said. "You have made me very hap-pee today. And tomorrow I shall talk with you from beyond la tombe."

I saw no point in cautioning her that her Ding would not be activated until she had died, which I did not anticipate would be as soon as tomorrow.

I was wrong.

Once she had been collected, she closed her eyes and died, a smile on her red lips.

I stayed in France long enough to sit with Mme. Constant's Ding and receive her assurance that she was pleased with the transition. My French was poor, but I believe she said, in broken English and Formal French, that she was ecstatic and that she hoped her closest friends would not be too delayed in joining her. Her compadore, a charming woman named Claire, smiled at me, and thanked me for coming. The downside to being CEO is that your own employees are reluctant to keep you around one minute longer than necessary.

***

Most newly activated Dings had been older than seventy, and nearly all had had physical issues when they were collected. Upon finding themselves in the Dingdom, and after the initial confusion and surprise wore off, the most common reaction was relief at their lack of pain.

"I used to pray that I could spend one day, just one day, without pain. In my mind, I still felt young, but my body wouldn't let me forget that I was old. And now ... I am reborn! I feel young and there's no part of me that hurts or is worn out." I heard words to this effect daily.

Chapter 13

Mendel Carver, Dar's late brother, shared several surprising revelations about his existence as a Ding. He approached his own arrival in the Dingdom as a researcher would, with detachment and detailed observation. He requested to meet with me, so I went to one of the Lounges and asked Craig, the compadore on duty, to take a break.

"Dings get tired of their compadores," said Mendel. "There is only so much small talk one can make, even with the most engaging compadore, before it becomes exasperating. I love Lisa, but with no more fulfilling relationship possible between us, I would just as soon not have her, or any of my compadores, visit with me anymore."

"They'll need to at least check in with you occasionally to see if you need anything."

"What can they get me that I would need?"

I asked him, "Do you talk with other Dings? Do they all feel this way?"

"I talk with some of them a little. Mostly I like to be by myself. I told a woman named Ann how I feel. She said she loves her compadores and would be lost without them. So maybe it's just me."

"Anything else you want to share?"

"The coolest thing about being a Ding is being part of the Internet, literally. I can explore anything I want anytime I want. I'm not traveling exactly, but I can immerse myself in other countries and other cultures, and it doesn't cost me a thing."

"What about language barriers?"

"There are none. I can get immediate translations of any page or text, and I can learn new languages instantly by appending them to my database."

"I never thought of that possibility," I said.

"You've no idea all the possibilities you created. I can even access the dark web… but I've learned why they call it 'dark'."

He seemed to get a sudden idea. "Hey, Declan, you know how Livings give everything a name? Every object, no matter how small, has a name, and every speck on the map, too, no matter how small. It turns out we Dings do the same thing. We've given names to all the places we go in the Dingdom, as you call it. For example, when we are summoned to a Lounge, we say we're going squinting. And when the cameras are turned off, we're in Darkoland."

"Oh, one other thing … Several Dings mentioned that the thing they miss the most is seeing sunrises and sunsets. I missed that, too, especially the dawn as darkness turns to light. So, I compiled a list of live cams around the world, and now we can watch anytime."

Mendel and I spoke for another thirty minutes. His experiences were fascinating and a little frightening. I would have to process them and determine if new policies might be needed.

Chapter 14

Dings were not allowed to work because it was determined that they would be ripe for exploitation. If a company could "hire" a Ding, there would be no way to pay them, so their labor could devolve into slave labor. Of course, the Ding could refuse to do the work, but what if the "employer" threatened the Ding's Living family?

Okay, that's an unlikely scenario, but what if the Ding voluntarily helped a company increase its productivity? Would Ding labor harm the economy by replacing Living employees?

When my father retired from his job in an insurance company, he was adrift for a couple of months. He drove my mother crazy because he didn't know what to do with himself. His best pal was still working, and Dad hated having nowhere to be during the day. In desperation, he bought himself a cheap guitar and started taking lessons. A week later, he bought a workbench and cleared space in the garage. "I won't need my car much anymore; it can sit out on the driveway."

Over the next few years, Dad found many new hobbies and outlets for self-expression. He became a model retiree.

It dawned on me that newly activated Dings were the same as my father. They were cut off from their daily routines and from friends they could go fishing with or meet for lunch. Dings need the opportunity to be active, and T.P. worked with compadores to develop an orientation program.

Most Dings adapted quickly, if not easily, to their new existence.

With the entire Internet at their command, they could keep their minds active indefinitely. However, two groups were the exception.

We found that athletes, including hikers, had the roughest transition from Living to Ding, followed closely by creative people for whom no outlet could be found in the Dingdom. Dancers and choreographers needed to discover new outlets for their expression. Musicians could still compose new songs, but there is no digital equivalent to, say, a violin. You can produce a violin-like sound synthetically, but a Ding cannot play an actual violin.

Unexpectedly, video producers thrived in the Dingdom. If they couldn't find a scene they wanted to use, they could create it through CGI, or they could talk Livings into producing and recording a scene.

Compadores suggested we create societies for various creative types. We did, and found they were instrumental in helping people adjust and learn how to flourish in the Dingdom.

Athletes were more difficult to acclimate. Their physically active lifestyles nourished more than their bodies; their mental health and sense of self benefited as well, and they thrived on competition. While some athletes had long ago slowed down with age, others had made a point of continuing to run or golf or otherwise stay fit. Taking that rush away meant that athletes took, on average, four more months to adapt than other Dings.

Take a professional footballer from Mexico called El Aguijón (the Stinger). For years, he was the most celebrated striker in the game, but he died at forty-five after a brief illness. He never adjusted to the Dingdom. He became moody and reclusive. He never asked to be terminated, but as far as I know, he never communicated with anyone, including his compadores.

Chapter 15

Clifton Heath was our youngest activated Ding. At nineteen, he was in a car accident that left him a quadriplegic. He died from complications of Covid-36 soon after his twenty-fourth birthday. He had been a handsome, athletic kid. A year after the accident, he returned to college and was near graduation when he got sick and died.

Aware he was dying, Clif arranged two things: he would be processed at a T.P. mobile facility, and he would marry his girlfriend and caretaker, Cathy Earnshaw. Cathy, twenty-one, was a shy, bookish woman studying to be a nurse. She wore no makeup and usually wore her dull brown hair piled in a spongy bun atop the back of her head. She had never dated, fearing she was too plain to interest boys her age. She had answered an ad to be a parttime caregiver to Clif, and they had slowly fallen in love.

Cathy was devastated when he died. He had been BRPed two days earlier, and we activated his Ding without waiting for the death certificate. He began asking for her as soon as he was online. We brought Cathy to the nearest Lounge a few hours later.

No one was happier to be a Ding than Clif Heath. "I feel like I got my body back," he told his compadore. "There's no more struggle to eat, no one pushing my bladder to make me pee, no one wiping my nose and my ass and my chin."

In a rare interview, Cathy told a reporter that sex with her husband had never been better. "He knows how to use his mind and his words to get us both excited. I can almost feel his hands on me when we're alone in the Lounge."

Cathy visited Clif almost daily for the next seventy years, until she joined him in the Dingdom. By then, he was still, effectively, twenty-four years old, while she was ninety-one.

***

The national media made a big deal about Clif Heath, Cathy, and what they dubbed "The Afterlife Romance." The attention prompted a flood of applications from people with various disabilities. Blind people wanted to know if they would be able to see once they were digital beings. I supposed that they would. I did not have to wait long to find out.

Carlotta Silverstone was a woman in her early eighties who had been blind since age six. She had seen almost nothing for three-quarters of a century. She said she was dying and wished to become a Ding so she could see again. Sensing a public relations bonanza for T.P., I dispatched one of our traveling BRP-mobiles to Carlotta's home in Sandusky, Ohio, and I went along.

Even in her dying hours, Carlotta was gracious and charming. Her mousy, dishwater gray hair looked like scrub grass in a dry Arizona desert, trying its best to stay alive. Her skin was cracked, and her fingers were bent and frail. Yet she was happy to see our crew, and excited to be collected. When we finished, she was almost giddy that the end of her physical struggles was days away at most.

By the time I returned to our North Waltham headquarters, Carlotta had passed. I felt privileged to be the one to activate her Ding and resurrect her to a new life. As soon as I did, her first request was to turn on the camera so she could see me.

"Oh my goodness! You're so handsome!" she exclaimed.

"I have a surprise for you, Carlotta," I told her. I had requested photographs of her at various ages from her family. From the digital album I had created, I presented them one at a time, and she got to see herself for the first time since she was a little girl. Each photo was captioned with helpful information. "That's your daughter, Josie," I said, "and here you are thirty years ago with your parents."

"They don't look anything like I remember them. They look so old. I have always thought of them as the thirty-year-olds I last saw. And me … I was prettier than I imagined, at least until I got old."

"You're still pretty, Carlotta," I told her.

"What about the world? Can you show me that? I always wanted to see the Louvre, and the Mona Lisa."

"It's all online. You can see everything."

"I had to die to live," she said. I never forgot those words.

Chapter 16

Dar told me on a Sunday evening that she was pregnant. I was stunned and reacted badly. I should have been supportive, but I said, "How could you do that?" I regretted my words instantly and spent the rest of the night trying to make up with her. By the next day, I accepted the fact that I'd be a father, and by Tuesday I was excited.

The doctors told Dar it would be considered a "geriatric pregnancy," which upset her. She was sick to her stomach for weeks and missed a lot of work. I did my best to take care of her, cooking the bland meals she would tolerate.

When she went into labor in her thirty-sixth week, she was convinced she was dying. She begged me to collect her. "I want to be with Mendel," she said. The obstetrician assured me she would not die. After thirty hours of labor, she delivered our son, Laz, by C-section. Mother and baby were both fine.

After Laz was born, I felt increasingly isolated socially. We named him Laz because his daddy raises people from the dead, but we thought "Lazarus" would be a shitty name to hang on a kid, not to mention it would be pretentious and open me to ridicule.

Other than my time with Dar, my life was consumed by my work. I wanted a social life and dreaded it as well. I realized I had kept few friends, and those I saw occasionally, such as Paul and Luna whom I knew from BU, required my initiation of contact. Friendships were work to me; I had to want them and pursue them, or they went nowhere.

Thanks to the incendiary Sen. Blather from Texas, I was now a marked man almost anywhere I went. I was accosted in the produce section at the supermarket by a woman who swung a bag of oranges at my back while shouting at me that I'd be going to Hell. Employees stocking bananas and broccoli pulled her off me and asked her to leave the store, but I left instead.

Another time, Dar and I were asked to leave a restaurant where we had just ordered our drinks because someone had seen us enter and organized a quick protest out front. The stress was taking its toll on Dar. We couldn't eat out, and we had no friends inviting us over, so each night became a routine of cooking and cleaning at home, and growing tired of the same meals. Having the baby did nothing to fix our isolation. Dar could take Laz out to the park or to coffee with a friend without incident, but her few friends rarely reached out.

Chapter 17

It would be physically impossible to BRP every person on Earth who dies each year. There would not be enough technicians, compadores, storage capacity, or money to cover the costs. Over 99 percent who die will not be preserved as a Ding. Decisions must be made about who is collected, and the only fair way to make those decisions is to have guidelines. A team of seven full-time employees reviewed every application and had the authority to accept or reject it.

We had appointed Chris Backoff, an attorney, as head of the Review Committee, an ombudsman-like team that would consider appeals of rejected applications.

When the Miller family—Tony and Sarah and their two children—came to us, they begged us to collect seven-year-old Emily, whose neuroblastoma was no longer responding to treatment. Sarah said, "We understand your policy is that people must be at least sisteen to be saved, but we ask you to make an exception in this case."

Chris explained that would be impossible. "Emily cannot give informed consent. She is too young to understand that she would literally be seven years old forever. She may continue to learn, but not to mature. She would lack all the experiences that would let her develop and be happy in a digital environment."

"How can that be worse than letting her die?" Sarah sobbed. "She will never have a chance to grow up, to go to prom, to fall in love, but she can still be with us, her family. She shouldn't lose her right to life just because she's not some arbitrary age." She gulped for air, then continued. "Look … we've coped with her illness for two years. We dealt with it when they told us she has the 11q aberration, putting her in the high-risk group. We've coped with everything that has been thrown at us, but I don't think I can cope with losing Emily."

Tony jumped in as Sarah choked up. "Emily understands what dying is. She has seen people from her cancer program die already. We love Emily more than you can know. We've been with her constantly for the past two years while she's been fighting really hard to stay alive. Perpetuonics gives us the chance to be with her even after her body surrenders to this shitty disease—pardon my French. Please give us that chance. We can pay whatever you want to charge."

"It's not a financial decision, Mr. and Mrs. Miller," Chris said patiently, even as he felt himself ready to crack. "We are bound by ethics and by provisions of the federal Protection of Digital Beings Act. It would be cruel to Emily to collect her and expect her to thrive."

The Millers left the meeting threatening to take it all the way to the Supreme Court, but they never went any farther, and the decision to reject Emily stood. She died two weeks later without being collected.

***

I had met the Most Reverend Michael Sorensen, a Catholic auxiliary bishop from the Archdiocese of Chicago, when I gave a speech at Loyola University on the Ethics and Morality of Creating Digital Beings. Sorensen spoke in opposition from a theological perspective. For example, he said, "God's desire for humanity is that it can draw near to Him, and He means that in a literal sense. Bodies are elemental, made of the same chemicals as the cosmos God created. Digital Beings—your 'Dings'—are not flesh nor are they are made in God's image. They cannot be saved. They cannot draw near to God. Psalm 42 says, 'My soul thirsts for God, for the living God; when shall I come and appear before God?' Tell me, Declan, how can a Digital Being appear before God?" He smiled as he fixed me with his gaze.

I smiled back and said, "A Ding is not dead, so I don't expect them to appear before God. Maybe the soul of the person they used to be will get that honor."

After the program, he and I continued our discussion with a small group of students and faculty, and we ended up hitting it off. I respected his concerns and attempted to address them calmly and rationally. He was extremely intelligent and knowledgeable about computer technology. We spoke by phone several times after I returned to Massachusetts.

I was surprised when he called me again a few months later and said he wanted me to accept his application for Dingdom. (I made a bad joke and asked if he wanted to enter the Dingdom of Heaven. He groaned.) I asked why he had changed his mind, and he told me that he had a terminal disease and was terrified at the prospect of a Judgment Day. He was proud of the life he had led, but he had not been perfect. He wondered if, as a Ding, he would forestall his personal purgatory, perhaps forever. I said I was not qualified to answer that question, but that no Ding to date had disclosed communicating with God or the Eternal.

We had recently opened a facility in Naperville, Illinois. I sent him there while he was still able to move about. They managed to get another collection of Michael closer to his passing. I never asked how he was able to afford both of his BRPs. I don't want to know that any more than I want to know what things he had done for which he feared judgment.

I visited Michael a few times after his Ding was activated. He was upbeat, serious, and philosophical about his new "life." He had resigned his position in the Church the same day of his first collection. He felt it was hypocritical of him to remain a Bishop and to preserve his soul through Twibil Perpetuonics instead of through the Catholic sacraments.

He confessed to me, "I had so much anxiety about dying. Every year, each birthday triggered increasingly morbid thoughts about how little time I had left. I was terrified every time I had trouble breathing or felt my heart race ... until I was collected. Then my fears went away. Suddenly, my death had an upside to it. I hadn't expected to become so calm and excited about my remaining time."

During my third and final visit with him, he confessed that he had started "seeing" a woman, another Ding named Esther Rosenblum. A Catholic priest and a noted Jewish feminist. What could go wrong? What might go right? In those early days of the Dingdom, we had so much to learn. A couple of universities introduced a new field called "ablolology," the study of abliving beings.

Chapter 18

As the Dingdom grew, we faced more issues surrounding love and marriage. The first Dings to request they be married were Noelle Mahler and Hiroshi Kunushiba. They shared a swing-shift compadore in our Denver facility, who introduced them. They discovered that they had met, briefly, at a party in Colorado Springs, and had several friends in common, though none of those friends was yet a Ding. Noelle was fifty-six when she died; Hiroshi was fifty-two. Noelle was a widow; Hiroshi's wife was still alive.

They spent entire days talking with each other. They declared that they were soulmates destined to be together. When they asked the compadore if they could get married, she told her manager, who kicked it up to T.P.'s policy panel. I sat in on their deliberations.

The request raised legal and ethical concerns, not the least of which was what would happen to Hiroshi's Living wife. There was no precedent in civil law.

When a living person's spouse died, the marriage was over as far as the law was concerned. The survivor could no longer file a tax return for a married couple, for example. One widower whose wife became a Ding claimed, unsuccessfully, that because he could still visit her, he should be allowed to file a joint return. The widower did not push it, so no court had yet ruled whether a marriage continued if one partner became a Ding. That was the closest case we could find to guide the policy panel.

Hiroshi told his Living wife that he had found a new love in the Dingdom. She cried. He asked her for a divorce. She got a lawyer who went to court and got an injunction against Hiroshi getting married. The news media had a field day with it. "Dead Man Wants to Get Married" said one headline. "I'll Give You a Divorce Over Your Dead Body" was how a tabloid covered it.

With everything held up in court, T.P. had no choice but to deny Hiroshi's request, but that hardly solved the problem. What if he were single? Would he be able to get married to Noelle then? Would such a marriage have any legal status? What would marriage between two Dings look like or mean? Clearly, there would be no consummation.

The next marriage proposal added to the confusion. Soon after we opened our Beirut facility, the first in the Middle East, we faced an impossible situation involving two Dings who had been women. Lila Abramian, a Christian who was seventy-seven when she died, wanted to marry Yasmina El-Yafi, a Muslim woman who had been eighty-one. Yasmina's Living children objected on religious grounds. The staff in Beirut began receiving death threats.

After several contentious meetings, the policy panel voted to ban marriage between Dings unless they were legally married to each other while living. Marriage, we reasoned, is a legal contract, and Dings had no right to execute legal contracts of any kind. Unofficially, compadores told would-be spouses that there was nothing that prevented them from declaring their love for each other and making commitments between them, but there could be no marriage certificate provided. Rumors began to float around that several Dings held secret commitment ceremonies.

The next crisis arose when a Ding couple—Rosa and Eduardo Gonzalez—had "marital difficulties." Eduardo was spending more time with a "younger woman" he met in a Latino society, and Rosa was angry. She accused him of adultery. The compadore had to explain that was not possible, but Rosa insisted it didn't matter if they were having "the sex." She still considered it grounds for divorce.

In the end, we decided we could not force them to stay together. Any Ding could block any other Ding from communicating with them, so we allowed Dings to declare a divorce, though we were assured that it had no legal standing, since officially, they were both dead.

***

A reporter from *Wired* was doing a story about perpetuonics, and Twibil wanted me to cooperate "as fully as possible" for the piece. A young guy originally from Finland with the great name of Miko Kokko called me with dozens of questions.

One question stood out. He wanted to know why Dings retained the same mental skills as when they were living. "Why couldn't T.P. use A.I. programmers to improve the intelligence of a Ding, making each one as 'smart' as every other Ding?"

I told him that would be unethical, even if it were technically possible, which is questionable. "I've talked with many Dings, and they unanimously oppose T.P. having control over their personalities and abilities."

He seemed disappointed in what he got from me. He was looking for a new angle that hadn't been covered before. He ended up writing a nice piece, and my corporate overseers were pleased. They would have been less satisfied if I had told the reporter my suspicions that Dings might learn how to evolve to higher intelligence without our interference.

Chapter 19

Laz, my son with Dar, was now almost twenty-two months. He was bright and happy. I wanted to spend every possible minute with him. After enduring each day confronting death, Laz gave me a chance to savor new life.

He had his mother's wavy brown hair and her large dark eyes, but he had my chin—minus the stubble, of course. I could always get one of his infectious belly-laughs if I threw a towel or blanket or napkin over his head and then yanked it away while squealing "Whee!" I don't know why he never tired of that game, but so far, it was his favorite.

Each day after work, I would take Laz to the playground near our house while Dar prepared dinner. On the swings, I would tell him to kiss the sky like Jimi Hendrix, and he would tilt his little round head back and throw kisses to the sky. He liked to take his green scooter and race around the small track and say "Choo choo!" I'd ask him if he was having a good time, and he said, "Laz good time." Then we'd go home, and the house would smell like curry or omelets or onions, and the three of us would eat together and talk until I took Laz upstairs for his bath and a story.

These rituals were beloved by Laz, and they were essential for me. As T.P. grew, there was tremendous pressure on me to work long hours and do everything possible to increase shareholder value. Yet I resisted successfully, because I could point to my little son and insist that my time with him was non-negotiable.

If need be, I would return to the office after putting Laz to bed. I was damned if I was going to let him grow up fatherless. My commitments to T.P. and to Laz left Dar precious little of my time. All I could do was promise her that it would not always be this way. But for now, I owed it to myself as well as Twibil to make perpetuonics a viable, permanent technology.

It was up to me to do what the history books would record about digitizing humans. Whether it failed or succeeded, my name would be the one listed first. With as much humility as I could muster, I knew I was the Father of Perpetuonics. I adored my wife and my son, but my passion was preserving humanity benevolently and sustainably. I'd even been considered for Time's Person of the Year, an honor that moved me more than I'd expected.

***

"What's bothering you?" Dar asked me one night when I got home too late to put Laz to bed.

"I ... collected myself today."

"You what?"

"I was curious, after all these years. I'd never done it before."

"Why now, then?"

"I don't know."

"You better not be fixing to leave me with this boy of ours. I can't do this without you."

"That's not why I did it."

"So ... why?

"I spend at least part of every day with people who are dying or who have already died. It's on my mind all the time."

"That doesn't sound healthy," Dar said.

"It's my job. It's my mission in life. I don't want to change it."

"Maybe you need counseling?"

"Maybe, but ... well, I'm all right. I'll be all right. I needed to collect myself. I see too many people who waited too long."

Dar got up from the swivel chair in which she'd been sewing when I came in. She hugged me tightly. "I'm a little confused, but okay. What are you going to do with it?"

"With my Ding? I don't know. Nothing, probably. Maybe I'll activate it to see what that's like."

"That's against your own policies."

"I know. I'll ... wait and see."

Chapter 20

Nancy Cosay was only thirty-eight when she died. She had Apache roots, though her mother was mostly Irish. Nancy had been stricken with lupus in her teens, but managed to survive twenty-one years despite frequent hospitalizations, chronic pain, and general weakness. Her parents, founders of a chain of clothing stores, had the financial means to have Nancy collected between hospital stays. They were with her when she died, and immediately contacted T.P. to activate Nancy's Ding. At their request, I met with Nancy, who "lived" at one of our New Jersey Perpetual Care facilities.

"I want a baby," Nancy told me. "For the first time in decades, I have no pain and I can think more clearly than I have since I was a child."

Nothing had surprised me more since I was six when a magician at a county fair pulled a live rabbit out of my shirt. Not much could surprise me after meeting so many Dings or applicants. Still, Nancy's request was a new one.

"You may feel like you still have a body, but you know that there is no physical you. How could you give birth to a baby?"

She smiled warmly, and I knew she was about to school me. "I did not say I want to create a baby, Mr. Marchand. I want to have one who will look to me as its mother."

"We don't allow babies to become Dings. The minimum age we'll accept is sixteen."

"I don't want a Ding. I want a real live baby to care for. I never had the chance to be a mother when I was alive. I never had a boyfriend for very long, and even if I did, I could not get pregnant. Ever since I was a little girl, I wanted to be a mommy. Now I'm ready."

I wanted to cry. My heart was breaking for her. I couldn't see any way to honor her request, but I didn't want to crush her dream immediately. "Let me talk to some people and see what we can work out," I said.

When I left the Lounge, I tried to think of something positive we could do for Nancy. She was going to be a Ding forever, and we wanted her to be content, if not enthusiastic.

Could we house a baby in a facility where human hands would follow Nancy's directions? "Why human hands?" I asked myself. Robots could do amazing things, including many with artificial intelligence. Why couldn't a robot change a baby's diaper and dress the kid? A Ding could easily send instructions to a robot.

The possibilities began to intrigue me. Technically, it seemed likely that a series of Ding-controlled robots could meet the physical needs of a baby. That left the emotional needs to consider. Is it ethical to deny a human baby the touch of a human caregiver?

That night at dinner, I told Dar about Nancy's request. She said, "There are lots of robots in daycare centers, but maybe not exactly what you're thinking of."

"What do the robots do? Are there any centers that are entirely robotic?"

Dar said, "Not in this country. I don't know about elsewhere. The robots here are mainly used for entertainment and education. The human caregiver can be taking care of a little one, like changing a diaper, while the robot keeps on eye on the other toddlers."

I shook my head. "I wouldn't want a machine taking care of Laz."

"It's no different than when you plunk him down in front of the TV so you can do something else."

I spent the rest of the evening doing research. I learned about Harry Harlow's monkeys in the 1950s, and how he showed that primate babies (presumably like humans) crave a soft cloth-wrapped robot versus a wire robotic "monkey" that provides only food and water. I watched videos of robots being used in daycare centers, and I watched a psychologist give a lecture about babies' needs for human interaction to develop healthy behaviors.

Over the next five days, I made a few phone calls. Early the next week, after calling in some favors, I had a plan in place. At 2:00 p.m., I met again with Nancy.

"I have great news, Nancy. We've made arrangements for you to foster a baby."

"Foster? But I want to adopt."

I stared directly at the camera. "That's never going to be possible. The law is clear; a Ding cannot enter into legal contracts, and adoption is a legally binding contract."

"And fostering isn't?"

"Normally it is, but our attorneys got an emergency hearing before a judge who agreed that a foster-care arrangement can be done by verbal agreement, recorded for the court. The judge said he would apply the same standards to you as a foster parent who has a severe disability. Like any foster parent, including a Living one, you will have no family relationship with the child and no rights regarding the child's future."

"Then the baby isn't really mine," she whined.

I wanted to be kind but firm. "It's not physically possible for you to have a child, and it's not legally possible for you to adopt one. Fostering Felicia is the best option for you.

"Felicia? You already have a baby for me?"

I had predicted she would be opposed to fostering unless we offered her a baby. "Would you like to see her? She's about one week old. Her birth mother, who lives on a reservation, rejected her, and no one has come forward to adopt her. She's about to go into the foster-care system."

Without hesitation, Nancy said, "Yes. Yes! I want to see her. Please. Oh my God."

I typed a command, and a video camera in a nursery came to life. Paula, a woman in a robin's-egg-blue uniform, was holding a tiny baby swaddled in a white cotton blanket with its tiny brown face peering at the camera. "Nancy, meet Felicia. Paula, I want you to meet Nancy. Nancy is the Digital Being who died last month, the woman I told you about this morning."

Paula waved. "Hi, Nancy. I'm here to help you take care of Felicia."

Nancy was smitten, and nearly speechless. She stared silently at the baby for a full minute. "I wish I could touch her," she confessed at last. "I love her. But if I have no legal rights, can't they take her away from me?"

"That's the deal with foster care," I explained. "However, I've been told that it will take at least a year for the authorities to assess how Felicia does in your care. You will be responsible every day for directing Felicia's care. The baby will live in a homelike environment provided by my company free of charge to you. We've already found a place in the baby's home state. Paula and a team of five others will take shifts being with Felicia and doing whatever you tell them to do. You get to pick out Felicia's clothing, and brand of diapers, and her physical activities."

Nancy was so excited. "And I never have to sleep, so I can keep Felicia company anytime she's awake! I'll be better than her real mother."

"So," I asked, "do we have a deal?"

Chapter 21

Achara Busarakham had been one of my favorite professors at BU, where I took her course on Asian Philosophy. She was a first-generation Thai-American. She was brilliant, with a wicked dry sense of humor. I adored her class, and intended to keep up with her after graduation, but it didn't happen.

Dr. Busa, as we called her, was petite, and seemed even smaller because her head barely rose above her shoulders. She had copper-colored skin and dark, curly hair. She liked to wear black pants and a shirt with a single, saturated secondary color, such as teal or orange.

I learned from a friend that Dr. Busa had retired due to failing health. I doubted she had the capacity to afford collecting, but I wanted her, more than anyone I knew, to carry on as a Ding after death. So, I contacted her and met her at her Brookline home for afternoon tea. I was prepared to cover all the costs of her BRPing.

We spoke for over an hour, reminiscing briefly about Boston University, but mostly talking about the Red Sox, whom she loved. As I accepted my third cup of tea, it was time to tell her the reason for my visit. I was delighted to learn that she had followed my career and knew all about Twibil Perpetuonics. I did not have to explain the process or the benefits of collecting, so I focused on the costs and how I wanted to help her.

"Mr. Marchand," she said to me, "life is so damned fleeting, but I honestly don't think I would want it to be any longer. So, no, thank you. I prefer to return my soul to the oblivion from which it sprang. I will not become one of your digital beings."

I have never felt so conflicted in my life. I was at once sad that her life would end and that I would not have the privilege of connecting further with her, and awestruck at the radiant courage she showed. I had always thought that every person, given the opportunity, would want to be a Ding and experience new life. She showed me a new approach to death.

***

Dr. Busa's refusal to accept a free ride to eternal life was a wake-up call to me. How many people would follow her example? More disturbing was the financial side of my enterprise. With few exceptions, only wealthy people would inhabit the Dingdom. While it was true that their past wealth would be worthless to them now—they could not take it with them—nearly every Ding would be someone who came from privilege. What kind of a "society was I creating? I resolved to find ways to collect a broader cross-section of the population.

I decided to create the Marchand Foundation. The invention of Dings had made me wealthy. Using half the money Twibil Biotech had paid me years before, I pledged $100 million to my charity with the intention of supporting people who lacked the means of collecting.

Jorge Sampedro was precisely the kind of person I had in mind when I created the Foundation.

Jorge, who lived in Santa Fe, New Mexico, was a sculptor. He supplemented his meager income with jewelry he made with copper and turquoise. Gifted and hard-working, Jorge lived in poverty. At age sixty-three, he had no health insurance and did not yet qualify for Medicare. When he began to cough up blood, he could not afford to go to the local clinic, so he ignored it and carried on until it was too late.

He heard about my foundation through a tourist who had bought some of his sculptures a couple of years ago and returned to buy more. Jorge applied for assistance to become a Ding, and he was accepted. We flew him to the nearest facility and collected him less than two months before he died in the same house where he grew up, and on the same bed where his mother had died ten years earlier.

I spoke with Jorge's Ding about a month later. He was lonely. None of his family could afford to travel to a Lounge, and he was generally ignored by some of his fellow Dings, who found nothing in common. His daytime compadore, Nathan, told me that loneliness was a major problem for Jorge and a few of Nathan's other Dings. Of all the problems I anticipated, loneliness never made the list. We then altered the Foundation's policies to support family visits in addition to collection costs. I paid personally for Jorge's wife and children to fly to Los Angeles and spend several nights in a hotel near the facility. They had a private Lounge all to themselves for three days. At least one of them came to visit him every couple of months until we opened a new facility two years later a few miles east of Los Alamos.

Despite his humble existence, Jorge found that many of the high-and-mighty Dings whom he encountered were excited to befriend him. His closest friends were an arts patron from Manhattan and a real-estate tycoon from San Francisco. I don't know what they found to talk about; it was impolite for a Living to eavesdrop, as it were. But Jorge's compadores reported that he was ebullient and prone to sharing gems of wisdom daily.

***

Agatha Jensema was one of the first women on a Major League Baseball team. She was a left-handed pitcher who'd learned to throw a wicked knuckleball. The Red Sox drafted her out of college and called her up mid-season from their Worcester farm team. As predicted, she got tons of hate mail and death threats. As a precaution, she decided to use some of her signing bonus and have herself collected by T.P.

When her Ding was activated, her compadores called me in to resolve an issue. Agatha had no idea how she died. During her initial orientation in the Dingdom, she remembered getting a threatening message the same morning she was collected. She asked if an angry fan had killed her. The compadore did not know whether to tell her the truth: she was murdered by her best friend, who thought—wrongly—that Agatha was "sleeping" with her husband. The compadores asked me whether to tell her the truth.

"You've got to tell her what really happened," I said without hesitation. "I read about the murder already. She's bound to find out soon, from online reports or from a visitor. Always be honest with your Dings; you need their complete trust."

I can't believe they didn't know.

***

"Only by facing down death do I feel truly alive," said Andy Adinolfi to a reporter shortly before he was killed while wingsuit flying in Norway.

Andy, a wealthy investment banker from Jersey City, was young, single, and bored when he paid Twibil millions to be collected, after which he immediately began indulging his extreme-sports obsession. He said he had avoided the dangers to which he found himself attracted until he realized that perpetuonics would eliminate the risk. I tried to advise him about taking unnecessary chances.

Within six months, he had run with the bulls in Pamplona, trained for free diving, taken a NASCAR driving course, climbed Mt. Rainier, begun training for Denali, and tried his hand at BASE jumping. After two weeks jumping in Norway, he was fascinated to try wingsuit flying. He smashed into a cold, remote fjord wall going 60 miles per hour.

When he was activated and oriented, he asked for me. "Am I really a Ding now? My plan worked?"

"Yes, it seems to have worked. You managed to kill yourself," I said matter-of-factly.

Andy was perplexed. "What do you mean, I killed myself?"

"Well, not like a deliberate suicide, but you died trying to fly in a wingsuit in Norway." Then I told him some of the other things he had done.

"Wait, so I did all those things? I really did them? Then how come I don't remember any of it?"

I took a deep breath. "Because your Ding was collected while you were still working. You hadn't done any of those things yet."

"Oh my God," he moaned. "I gave up my life to do all those things I'd dreamed of doing, and now I'll never remember any of it? It's like I never did them."

Within two days, we heard from Andy's attorney, demanding that we terminate Andy's Ding. He no longer wished to be activated, and he released us from our contract. Our lawyers gave us the green light, and we let Andy go into that great dark matter. We kept his millions.

Chapter 22

One of my happiest childhood memories was the day my father got wireless speakers set up throughout our house. Dad was always listening to music on StupefyPro, the service that guaranteed musicians a fair share per play. It was Dad's one luxury. I must have been ten or eleven. Dad made me sit quietly for an hour while he played me his favorite songs. I would have been bored to tears, but I felt happy seeing Dad as full of joy as ever.

He played "Uncle Joe" by his current favorite singer, Scaramouche. Then he went on a songs-about-uncles binge and skipped through Paul McCartney's "Uncle Albert / Admiral Halsey," "Uncle Jack" by Spirit, and "Uncle John's Band" by the Grateful Dead, which I had never heard before and totally loved. He made me listen to "Sweet on You" by the Black Mountain Pumpboys, and "Let Me Down Forever" by Taylor Swift. That led to a montage of old songs about death and dying: "Tears in Heaven" by Eric Clapton, "Don't Fear the Reaper" by Blue Oyster Cult, and "Soul Meets Body" by Death Cab for Cutie. That song closed the "show." He'd had enough and sent me to my room to do homework.

***

Shortly before Laz's second birthday, Dar and I flew with him to Tel Aviv for the opening of our first T.P. facility in the Middle East. The Israeli government lobbied hard to bring perpetuonics there, and our Board agreed, now that the Palestinians had been granted complete autonomy and self-rule.

I received VIP treatment when we landed. The Prime Minister greeted us at the airport and took us by limousine to our hotel on the Mediterranean.

The number of Israelis who had registered to be processed was staggering. We were told that, in part, it's because Jews are less concerned about an afterlife than Christians are. In the States, few evangelical Christians were being collected for fear they would be in a sort of purgatory, no longer alive but not able to enter the Kingdom of Heaven. It seems that none of them thought they might be going elsewhere after death.

It was Dar's and my first real vacation since Laz was born, and we aimed to take maximum advantage of our situation. When I was not at the new T.P. building in Ramat HaSharon on the outskirts of Tel Aviv, we spent most of our time at the beach. Laz loved splashing in the gentle waves outside our hotel. I took dozens of photos of him.

One day when I had to spend hours at the facility, Dar took our sweet boy by train to Jerusalem. She climbed to the Temple Mount and the Dome of the Rock with him and tried to impress him with the size and age of the building, but all he wanted to do was drag his fingertips through the ancient dust and rub it on his tummy.

We also took him to see the Dead Sea. I told him there was so much salt in the water, he could not sink. So, he threw himself into the water and immediately sank, coughing and spluttering and crying at the same time. We rinsed the salt off his face and out of his hair, laughing gently at his distress. He did not fully trust us the rest of the trip.

***

Tommy Hatch was loaded (in both senses of the word) when he was a Living. He had more money than he knew what to do with, and he was always drunk.

He got through the pre-collection screening because we tested for drug use, but not for alcoholism. It bothered me to institute the drug tests, but our Board reasoned that people whose mental ability to cope with life depended on cannabis or other psychotropic drugs would find life in the Dingdom excruciating. I couldn't prove the Board wrong, and I didn't want to experiment with anyone's Ding in case they were right.

Tommy was a B-list celebrity rock star. He had made a fortune playing lead guitar with a band that had a couple of platinum albums in the '30s. He had used his lanky bad-boy good looks to be featured in a couple of reality TV series, but he got a reputation for being hard to work with, perpetually late, and often smashed on set. No one was surprised when he failed to wake up one morning in an Atlanta hotel, but I was surprised to learn that he had been collected In Kuala Lumpur, and his Ding had been activated.

It wasn't long before his compadore asked me to talk with Tommy, who was insisting on being supplied with cocaine and single-malt Scotch. Apparently, he could not comprehend the difference between his former life and the Dingdom. All he knew was …

"I don't have a body. So what? Since when do you need a body to feel good?"

"Tommy," I said, "I know your brain feels like it always did, but drugs and alcohol affected your mood by changing your body chemistry, and now that you're a Ding, you don't have any chemicals we can alter. It doesn't work like that."

"I have no fucking idea what you're talking about," Tommy said.

"You don't have any—"

"Never mind!" he interrupted. "What about girls? Can you get me girls? What do you call 'em here?"

"They're still called 'girls,' and they're not something we provide."

"Stupid mistake," he mocked. "You'd get a lot more people

here if you had girls."

"Thank you for that great advice," I said. He did not notice I was not serious.

"Listen, man; you're a cool dude. Optimal! You know what I'm talking about. See what you can do for me, okay?"

"I'll look into it, Tommy," I said, knowing there was nothing to look into. I imagined Tommy was not going to adapt well to existence in the Dingdom. I never checked back.

Chapter 23

As we opened more facilities, and as the number of Dings grew rapidly from a few dozen to a few thousand, we learned more about the Dingdom.

No Ding remembered dying. Even those who were on the cusp of death were collected before the actual moment, and therefore had no memory of passing. That disappointed clergy and philosophers who wished to know exactly what happened at that final instant of life. People went from being alive to being digital with no recollection of the transition.

Dings found new outlets for their passions. Writers could write non-stop, since they had no need to pause to eat or sleep. We had five Nobel Prize winners in the first three years alone, and one best-selling author of romantic fiction. Literary agents flocked to Lounges to sign up dead authors and showcase their new works. Living authors were nearly abandoned.

Sam Rockwell, considered by many to be the finest American actor of the twenty-first century, was collected shortly before he died at eighty-four. He had finally won a Best Actor Oscar™ for his role as Senator Sam Ervin in a new story about the old, mid-twentieth-century Watergate scandal. Sam organized a group of Ding actors into a repertory company, performing works of Shakespeare, O'Neill, and other great playwrights. With no physical limitations, they found they could each take on almost any role, and with unlimited memory at their disposal, learning lines took no time at all.

Even painters got in on the act. They could not manipulate a paintbrush, but with digital tools, they could create phenomenal works of extraordinary imagination. The Dingdom was proving to be a fertile incubator of artistic expression.

***

One of the most fascinating early Dings was Trevor Shoals. Trevor was a British author of a series of popular murder mysteries, most of them featuring a detective named Zazu Adebayo, who solved cases in Birmingham, a city about which I knew nothing except that it was in the middle of England. I never met Trevor while he was living.

Trevor had been a bricklayer, a property manager, and an estate agent before he published his first novel, an instant classic named "The Shadow Doesn't Lie." After that, he had married, raised three children, and become one of the wealthiest men in England. He researched his stories meticulously, learning all he could about police procedures and forensic pathology.

I received a call on Thursday morning from the manager of our Manchester, England, facility. He asked me to talk with Rita, one of his compadores. She said I should go online and talk with Trevor Shoals, and she gave me his ID. I asked her why I would want to talk with him, since it was an unusual request. Rarely did we allow anyone other than family members and compadores to speak with a Ding. Rita said, "I'll let Trevor tell you. He's kind of peculiar. He's up to something."

I found a vacant Lounge and rang Trevor. When he accepted my call, his animated avatar popped up on the screen. "Hi, Trevor. My name is Declan Marchand. I'm the—"

"I know who you are," he rasped. "I may know more about you than you do."

Ignoring his threatening tone, I said, "Why did Rita tell me to talk with you? Is there something wrong?"

"Not with me, there's not."

"With someone else, then?"

"What do you know about me, Declan?"

"Not much, to be honest. You're an author, right?"

"Right. Murder mysteries, mostly."

"So, what's going on?" I asked, anxious to get to the point.

"I know a great deal about investigating a murder, and now, at last, I'm in a position to do something about it."

"What do you mean?"

"I mean I can easily gather data the police can't get. Sometimes I can access cameras in people's homes and offices. I can see their emails and bank records and all kinds of things they don't want the detectives to see. I know what to look for and how to find it."

"That sounds sketchy to me, Trevor. It's illegal."

"No, it's not. I'm not a copper. I don't need a warrant. Anyway, no one can stop me, and they can't know what I'm doing unless I want them to know."

I was losing my patience. "So, what do you want from me?"

"I don't want anything from you. You called me, remember?"

"Rita said —"

"Rita is sweet, but she's naïve. I shouldn't have told her anything."

"It sounds to me like you're proud of what you're doing."

"You bet I am," Trevor said. "I could only fantasize about being a detective when I was a Living. Now I can do more than any detective. I can solve murders they'd never figure out. I'll be the greatest crime solver in history. I already am."

"Not if I pull the plug on you."

"Why would you do that? I'm one of the good guys."

"How do I know that? With your power, you could do a lot of harm."

"You insult me, Mr. Marchand. I want what the police want, to catch the bad guys."

"By circumventing the law."

"Oh please. You're as naïve as Rita. Every inspector I ever knew would give anything to do what I can do." He paused. "I'll tell you what. I promise only to investigate when the CID is stumped."

"The CID?"

"The Criminal Investigation Department. Those are the guys who get the hardest cases."

"But you're not responsible to anybody."

"I know! I'm living the dream."

I was tempted to remind him that he's not living at all, but coming from me, that would hardly be appropriate.

"Can I assume you've already begun this work?" I asked.

Trevor said, "Of course. I've helped authorities solve two unrelated murders this week."

"Is crime that bad where you are?"

"Where am I, Declan? Where am I? I'm everywhere. Who said I would investigate crimes only in England? As it happens, I'm working on a case that has Chicago police stumped, and I'm thinking of taking on a case in Brisbane."

For the next fifteen minutes, Trevor and I conversed about the cases he was following, what he had discovered and turned over to local police, and how thrilled he was to be able to go around the world. He complained that he could not interact with others the same way he and I were communicating. He wanted to be able to talk through speakers and display his evidence on their screens. Twibil Perpetuonics had made sure that Dings would be accessible only through our facilities.

I knew then we would have to revise our policies. T.P. could become a gatekeeper, allowing outsiders access to our Dings only by approval. A Ding could appeal if we blocked the outsider who requested access, but the final decision had to rest with T.P.

Trevor had been obliged to reach out to authorities through emails. He had created his own email account and, with the help of a Ding who'd been a technology wizard, had turned his own server into an email hub that was, like Trevor, completely anonymous and invisible to search engines and to ICANN, the international agency that oversees Internet Protocol. The best he could do was to send detailed tips to investigators and hope they would take it seriously. He signed his messages "Gilbert Ryle," the philosopher who had coined the phrase "Ghost in the Machine" and opined on the separation of mind and body.

Later that day, I contacted a friend at the *Chicago Sun-Times*. He confirmed that police there had recently solved the cold-case murder of Sean Mistral-Jones after receiving an anonymous tip. He later confirmed that the tip had come from someone supposedly named Gilbert Ryle, that police concluded it was not a real person, and they questioned my friend for a couple of hours trying to find out what he knew about the tipster.

"Becoming a Ding is the best thing that ever happened to me," said Trevor. "I get to do everything I love, and I don't have to clean up after myself. I never need a warrant, and no one is shooting at me. Best of all, I'm writing again. I was too sick the last two years to do anything, and now I can crank out a new book every week. I was never keen on the money side of things, you know, and now it doesn't matter. I don't have to sit in horrid, musky bookstores and sign my books for semi-literate blighters. And deadlines! No more deadlines!"

"I'm glad it suits you, Trevor. I always love to hear of our success stories."

"Cheers, mate! Oh, and give that lovely Rita a raise, will you? She's the fyrverk." (I had to look that one up, since I knew little about British slang.)

Before we parted, I had to ask Trevor a question. "When you were alive, did you have a raspy voice?"

He laughed. "No, my voice was kind of high-pitched, to tell the truth. But when they gave me a choice of voices for my Ding, this is how I wanted to sound."

***

Trevor, it seemed, was one of the more benign characters we had collected. He was trying to be helpful in his unconstrained way. Other Dings were discovering the freedom they had gained, not the least of which was freedom from legal consequences, a weakness we would come to regret.

We had anticipated the need to constrain direct communications between Dings and Livings, but we overlooked Dings' ability to write whatever they wanted and to broadcast it widely. It did not take long for Dings to flood social media with commentary using aliases that were untraceable. While many tried to spread the "truth" as they understood it, a growing number of Dings enjoyed lying outright, making up outrageous disinformation.

I called an emergency meeting of our top management from all over the world. We had a full-blown crisis on our hands, and if we did not address it, we would soon find ourselves in courtrooms everywhere.

By now, Twibil had assembled a large team of computer specialists to keep our servers running and our many client services operating smoothly. T.P. had progressed a long way from my little Cambridge lab. We directed the team to drop everything non-critical and rework the abilities of the Dings everywhere.

Dings would no longer be able to sub-out their own servers. Those servers were to contain nothing but a Ding's own BRP profile. If a Ding wanted an email address, T.P. would provide it to them, and it would be monitored by the compadores. We expected the Dings would object to what they perceived as an invasion of their privacy, but they had no recourse. The freedom they enjoyed from consequences for their misdeeds also kept them from asking the courts for redress of their grievances.

Dings were henceforth to have no access to any social media used by Livings. We explicitly named all the known platforms, and said the rule would extend to future platforms as well. We had, by then, found several instances of a Ding who had spread disinformation intended to swing an election. The last thing we needed was abliving people controlling how living people would be governed.

Our marketing department put together a five-minute video explaining the new policies and giving specific examples—minus anyone's name—of why the rules were needed. We would share this information with the public and especially with anyone applying to be collected.

***

Someone wrote to T.P. and asked, "Are there virgins in the Dingdom?" What a strange thought to have.

So, I answered, "Does it matter whether a Ding knows what sexual intercourse feels like? Dings are no longer concerned with what bodies can do. We don't allow anyone younger than sixteen to become a Ding. The average age of Dings so far is about sixty-three, which means they were mature adults. Mature adults don't expect others their age to be virgins, so it's not something we ask about."

The notion of "virgins" seems like a relic from the past. Why do we divide people by whether they've had intercourse? That seems to belong to ancient religions, not to the Livings of the twenty-first century. Only adolescents worry about it. Does this guy really imagine he could "deflower" some innocent Ding after he's BRPed?

Chapter 24

I got a call from the CEO at Twibil Biotech, our parent company. "Gideon Calhoun just died," he said with a trace of sadness in his voice.

"The evangelist?" I asked.

"Yep. He was a good friend to my wife and me. I secretly helped him be collected a few months ago. He didn't want his fans to know."

I was virtually in the Lounge to greet Gideon a few minutes after he was activated. He was confused, as most new Dings are. His compadore, a fifty-five-year-old man named James, was in the Lounge to help Gideon with orientation. Gideon was uncharacteristically quiet. Arrival in the Dingdom is a lot to take in, as I was to learn.

"Hello, Gideon," I said when the welcoming compadore stopped speaking. I know I should have called him "Reverend Calhoun," but at the last moment, that didn't feel right. "My name is Declan Marchand. I'm the founder of Twibil Perpetuonics. Welcome to the Dingdom." I paused to see if Gideon would respond. Five seconds later, he did.

"So, I'm dead?"

"Yes, you are. Your body is, anyway."

"Praise God! I can't believe it."

I smiled. "Actually, you can believe it, and you did, by acknowledging that you're now a Digital Being … a Ding."

"Where am I?"

"I'm talking to you in a Perpetual Care Center Lounge, the one in Kansas City where your Ding is stored. We activated you moments ago. Do you remember when you were collected?"

"It feels like that just happened," Gideon mused.

"To you, it happened moments ago, but that was actually several months back."

He was becoming more alert and focused. "I guess I won't ever know what happened in those months, will I? How did I die?"

"I don't know, uh …"

"You can call me Gideon, please."

"Gideon, I don't know. Apparently, you died a short time ago, and T.P. activated your Ding immediately. Wait a couple of days, and you'll be able to use the Internet to read your own obituaries."

"Oh my goodness! Really? That's amazing. And … I suppose if my funeral is televised, I could watch that, too?"

"Absolutely. You can probably watch it live."

"Imagine that! I'm dead and watching my own funeral as it happens. Remarkable!"

I gave him a moment for that realization to sink in. Then I said, "I have someone who's been waiting to meet you."

"Really? Waiting to … Someone I know."

"Someone you know very well. Or knew very well."

"Hi, Gideon," said a female voice.

"Celeste? Is that you?" he gasped.

"Oh, Gideon, I've missed you so."

Gideon was flabbergasted. "Declan, that's my wife, Celeste!" He choked with emotion.

"I'm going to leave you two alone to catch up," I said. "I'll check back in with you tomorrow." I disconnected from the conversation. I had seen a few other such reunions, and I knew they would not need me there to mediate.

The next afternoon, I reached out to Gideon again. He sounded calmer but no less ebullient. "I must say, Declan, it feels like I'm talking with God. I'm dead, yet I'm alive."

"That's a common feeling, Gideon."

"So, are you God now?"

I laughed. "No, not now, not ever. Not for you or anyone else."

"You are like a God, giving me a life after death. I wasn't always so sure I'd want that."

"You're kidding. You're Gideon Calhoun, preacher to millions. You've been telling people for generations how to get right with God. 'I'm God's Agent here on Earth.' I've seen clips of you saying that. Didn't you believe in Heaven? Didn't you want to believe?"

"I did … or at least, I used to. I wanted to believe in Heaven and that I was good enough to go there. But I've had my doubts for a long time now. Secret doubts. Only Celeste knew how I felt deep inside."

"How do you feel now?" I asked.

"I'm trying to work that out, Declan. I think maybe this is better than Heaven. That's what I hoped, before I asked to be collected."

"That's a heck of a message, coming from you."

"I wasn't thinking about sending a message. I was thinking about Celeste. She told me years ago that she wanted our souls to be together forever, and when she heard about perpetuonics, she said it would give us a chance for that. So, she got herself collected, quietly. Didn't tell any of our friends … or the leaders in my church, of course. When she died a couple of years ago, I talked with your CEO about me. I didn't want to wait too long to be collected, and when I got diagnosed a few months ago, I asked him to collect me in total confidence."

"He kept your secret all these months," I marveled. "No one has to know you're here except me and your compadores … and Celeste, of course. Although it's not normally done, you two will share the same compadores to help protect your privacy."

"That's wonderful. Celeste told me. Thank you."

"I'm sure she's excited to have you with her again."

Gideon paused. "Yes, we're both excited, but it's stranger than I expected. Celeste told me that she spent the past two years in isolation, waiting for me. It's as if she were in a coma, she said. And now she's only out of that coma because I died. She's equal parts sad that I died and happy to be conscious again. That's the most terrible paradox I can imagine."

I nodded and was about to respond when he launched into a new thought. "Virtually every living thing produces waste, but we Dings are an exception. Does that mean we're not alive? I feel like I'm alive, but I know that I'm not by any scientific definition. How am I supposed to reconcile myself to being not-alive? Usually, that would mean dead, but I'm not dead, either. The Dingdom is a third state of human existence. We had to live to acquire consciousness, and then we had to die to preserve it forever."

He continued, "Now of course, there is waste associated with the production of the electricity that storing a Ding consumes. Unlike plants and animals, electronic waste is non-organic. It's not scat. My existence has no carbon footprint. I am more ephemeral than a human. I'm like an angel ... or a ghost."

I was fascinated by Gideon's insights. He was experiencing the Dingdom in ways I had never predicted, and it all made sense. I realized that I should have spent more time talking with other Dings to see if these insights were universal.

Chapter 25

"The senator admired your work greatly," his wife told me as we entered a Lounge to speak with him together for the first time as a Ding. "He was excited to become a digital being."

Senator Mark Rasmussen of Minnesota had, indeed, been an ally when we needed congressional help. I had met him once at a hearing. He died a few days before I went to visit him.

"Declan!" he boomed when I stepped in front of the camera. "Tell me … how did I die?"

His wife, Kathy, answered for me. "You got hit by a car crossing D Street on your way to Union Station."

"You're kidding," he said.

"You were in a coma. Declan got here in time to collect you."

"Wow! That was pretty stupid of me. What happened to the driver?"

Kathy said, "Nothing. People saw you step off the curb right in front of him. I've always said you're too distracted."

"Well, I'm dead now, so maybe you can stop worrying about that. Hey, I wonder if I can still vote on legislation?"

"The governor already named your replacement. Linda Shoemaker."

"Oh no, not her!" he said. "She's useless."

"I think that's why he chose her. There will be a special election next year, and she promised not to run. Of course, I don't really trust her."

Mark said, "Neither do I. You should run, Kathy."

"Me? No thanks. Politics is your thing."

"Senator," I said, "I've got to get back to Massachusetts. I stopped in to pay my respects and see if you need anything."

"What could I need? I met that adorable little compadore you got me ... Zoey. She's taking good care of me. Hey, thanks for coming by, Declan. And thanks for collecting me."

I said I would check in with him from time to time, and he could send me messages if he needed something. Then I got a ride to the airport and headed home to Dar and Laz.

****

In October, some Dings formed a Halloween Society and expressed a desire to "dress up" for Halloween. They requested the right to substitute altered avatars of themselves or to show other images.

T.P.'s Standards Committee decided to allow specialty avatars under certain conditions:

- A "non-personal avatar" is any animated avatar that alters the appearance of a Ding so as to be unrecognizable;
- Like traditional personal avatars, non-personal avatars may not depict any body part other than a head and neck;
- Non-personal avatars must not include any text or symbols on the head or face;
- Non-personal avatars can be used no more than six days in a calendar year.

The committee was afraid that some Dings would go hog wild if there were no time limits. They didn't want to sow confusion among Dings.

That first Dingdom Halloween was a huge success. Many Dings from cultures that did not observe American Halloween customs were intrigued and joined in the fun. Dings with little artistic ability enlisted the help of Dings who were great at design, like Jorge Sampedro. He created wonderful costumes that reflected the more private lives of other Dings—the quirks, fantasies, memories they kept quiet but allowed to emerge for Halloween. We ended up with beautifully animated dragon heads talking with hideous "witches" and balloon-faced babies. I had never imagined the Dingdom could be such fun.

Chapter 26

A week or so later, I again visited Gideon. He described his last two years as a Living.

His physical self had been suffering from neuropathy and could not stand the itching without relief. He knew that he, like his parishioners, should have been excited about seeing God after his death, but doubts began to surface. He realized he would rather be a Ding than an angel, especially with Celeste already in the Dingdom.

Gideon told me how happy he is that he died before Christmas. The holiday wore him out physically and emotionally, although he added, "I miss the Christmas decorations. I'd like to find a way to decorate the Dingdom."

He went silent for a moment. As I pondered how we'd do that, he continued. "I want to come out of the closet, so to speak," Gideon revealed.

I was bewildered. "What do you mean?"

"I mean, I haven't told anyone, Living or Ding, that I'm here. It's confining, which I expected, and it's wrong, which I didn't expect."

"What do you mean, it's wrong?"

"I can't spend eternity avoiding everything ... well, avoiding the truth, anyway. God delivered Celeste and me to the Dingdom. We must recognize it for a miracle. The Dingdom is not instead of Heaven ... it is Heaven. "

"I wouldn't go that far," I cautioned him. "For one thing, it's not open to everyone. It's still quite exclusive."

"That can change," he assured me. "That will change. In years to come, anyone who wants eternal life will find their way to the Dingdom of Heaven."

"Is that what you think?" I asked. "I don't want Livings hearing that. We'll end up with mass suicides."

Again, he went silent. "You're right," he conceded after a moment. "I know how easily people can misconstrue a simple message. They think everything I say is a parable, when sometimes I am just talking about a good steak or a cute baby."

I laughed. "A cigar sometimes is just a cigar, right?"

Gideon laughed heartily. "You know, Freud never actually said that." I liked that he knew what I was talking about. There were many layers to this "man of the cloth," and it was fun to discover them.

Gideon continued. "Okay, I won't talk about Heaven when I communicate with Livings, but I do want to communicate with them. I want them to know I became a Ding. I'm not ashamed of it."

"You know what Senator Blather used to say about Dings, right?"

"We're an abomination. I know. I heard him say that, and I decided to let sleeping dogs lie. But I never agreed with him. And now I can use my voice to shut him up."

"I'd love it," I said.

Chapter 27

Radislav Mariescu was ranked #3 in the world of professional tennis when he got Covid and died. Only twenty-seven years old, he had earned more than $200 million in winnings and endorsements, but his star was tarnished when he refused to be vaccinated and was denied entry to the Australian Open and Wimbledon the year before he died.

He secretly arranged to be collected at our facility in Dubai during a tournament there. He could afford, he reasoned, to be collected every five years, a process that would involve bribing local T.P. employees.

I never met a bigger asshole. He tried to treat the Dingdom the same way he had treated the world of tennis and his fans: with disdain. He expected the compadores and the other Dings would defer to him and be starstruck. I began hearing complaints within hours of his activation.

Radislav believed he should be able to communicate with any Living person without conditions and without going through T.P. facilities. "I have millions of fans," he said, "maybe billions. I am the most loved man in the world. I could have been elected president of my country. You must let me talk to anyone who asks."

"That's not how it works here," I told him. "You accepted our terms when you were collected."

"I did not read all that tiny print. I was too important to waste my time."

I was unsympathetic. "It was not 'tiny print,' as you call it. It is one of the most important things we tell everyone who is collected. Dings must communicate with approved visitors in a Lounge. Without such control, chaos would quickly consume you and us."

Radislav complained, "I paid you millions of dollars. You cannot treat me like some peasant."

"There are no peasants in the Dingdom. No Ding is more powerful than any other. No one cares what you did before you died. Almost everyone here paid millions of dollars, too. Money has no value in the Dingdom."

"But it has value to you," he snarled. "Your rules can be bent."

"No, they can't. We have legal and ethical commitments, and no one is going to jail so you can feel special."

Chapter 28

Amanda Stevenson of Council Bluffs, Iowa, called a T.P. facility one Wednesday. She sounded desperate. Her forty-two-year-old husband, Steve, had suffered a stroke. He had been alone at home when it occurred. Now he was in the hospital, but his prognosis was poor. Amanda did not expect him to live another twenty-four hours. "I don't want to lose him. We're too young, and our kids need their daddy." She asked if we could process him before he passed. Ramon, the director of our Omaha facility, called me at home.

We had never BRPed such a recent stroke victim before. I had no idea how his Ding would be affected, but I dispatched a BRP-mobile to Steve's bedside. Amanda sat beside him as the technician collected Steve's soul and memories. He seemed unaware of the process. His wife held his hand, tears streaming down her cheeks as the machine whirred and purred. She never moved as the technician packed up the gear and silently left, and she stayed by Steve's bed the rest of the night. Minutes before 7:00 a.m., he died. His heart monitor flat-lined. Amanda stood, kissed his forehead, and went home to tell their children.

I was anxious to learn how the collection went. I returned to the Lounge where I had confronted Trevor Shoals, and I accessed Steve Stevenson.

"Hello, Steve. Can you hear me?"

"Huh?" came the reply.

"Steve, my name is Declan. Can you hear me? Can you speak to me?"

"Chicken."

"Did you say 'chicken,' Steve? What are you trying to say?" His first word was spoken in our default computer voice. I hit a few buttons and changed it to a higher pitch.

"Mommy. Chicken."

"I don't understand."

"Light bulb party in my chicken."

I brought my hand to my mouth. My eyes scanned the Lounge as I tried to comprehend what was happening. Had something gone wrong in the collection? Was this babble a glitch in the system, or was that all Steve was capable of?

Ramon was on the phone from Omaha. Amanda Stevenson was in his office, demanding access to her husband's Ding. What was the hold-up?

I instructed Ramon to tell Amanda gently that Steve's Ding was not accessible at this time, and that we had our team working on the problem. I promised to get back to him within an hour. Then I called our head of I.T. and asked her to meet me in the Lounge.

For the next hour, we tried everything we could think of to repair Steve's Ding. We even sent someone to check the original files from the hospital collection. The data were not corrupt; they were inadequate to the construction of a model of the man Steve had been. We concluded that Steve's brain had been too damaged by the stroke. There was still activity there at the time he was BRPed, but it was basically short circuited.

I called Ramon back and asked him to bring me up on video in his office so I could address Amanda directly.

"Ms. Stevenson—Amanda—I'm extremely sorry to tell you.... We've tried everything. You will not be able to talk with Steve. His brain was too badly affected by the stroke, and we were unable to achieve a viable digital being."

She tried valiantly to hold herself together, but I could see her shoulders shaking and her lips trying to form words that never came. "There's nothing? Isn't there a small part of him I could …" She paused and looked away from the screen with my face on it. "Did he suffer? Can you tell if he was suffering when you, you know, collected him?"

"As far as we can tell, he was unaware of anything. He was not suffering."

She whispered, "Oh, that's good; that's good."

"You have my deepest sympathy," I said.

"Okay, thank you. Thank you for trying. I guess … I'm a widow now. I told the kids there was hope, but … well, you tried. You tried." She began sobbing. "I tried, Steve. I tried to save you. I'm sorry."

She stood, and Ramon escorted her out of his office. The call ended. I wiped a few tears from my eyes.

Chapter 29

Rev. Gideon Calhoun was everywhere in the Dingdom. Compadores all over the world reported that their Dings were commenting about him. It was time for me to pay him another visit.

"Hello, Declan. It's good to see you again."

"Gideon. How've you been?"

"I haven't felt this alive since I was a young Living minister starting out in Stonecrest, Arkansas. I have more ideas and I never run out of energy!"

"That's great!" I said.

"And I can multitask like crazy. I'm talking to you, and at the same time, I'm running a seminar for something called the Digital Christians Society."

"Let me guess … you started that group."

"Ha. You're right. I saw so many Dings feeling cut off from religion. It had been a big part of their lives, and then suddenly it was almost a forbidden topic. No one was talking about it. A big part of religion is the gathering in community, not only for worship but for spiritual support. The Dingdom doesn't have physical churches or mosques or ashrams or temples, so Dings have been isolated. Anyone wanting religion has been shunned."

"No! Shunned? Really?"

"Yes! That's the right word for it. So many religious leaders demonized the Dingdom. People were afraid to be collected, so there are fewer deeply religious Dings here than there should be."

"Wow! Well, I guess you're the right man for the job." I was impressed.

"It's hard not to believe in God when you find yourself active after death. Dings are just waking up to that fact. I have a million-plus followers already, more than that Imam who was activated a year ago."

"Congratulations," I said. "You're obviously filling a need in the Dingdom."

I did not say what I'd been thinking: even in the Dingdom, Christians and Muslims will still compete. Dings will be tribal, identifying more with their own faith community than with their former race or nationality.

***

"Perpetuonics changed everything for me," said David Lodge as we met for coffee. He was one of my earliest investors and a member of my first Board of Directors. David was eighty-two years old, the patriarch of a branch of the venerable Lodge family, and one of the richest men in Massachusetts.

"Like most Livings, I didn't understand how old age changes a person. My whole adult life, I felt about thirty-five or forty. Even as my body aged, I felt young inside. Then one day—I think it was on my seventy-eighth birthday—I knew my ride was about over. My outlook on everything changed. I was old! Two years later, you came along with your offer to collect me, and suddenly, I was young again because I stopped thinking I was near the end. I could live any way I wanted, and I'd still be all right, either as a Living or as a Ding."

I smiled broadly. "I hope you live another twenty years, David, but when the time comes, you're going to love being a Ding." He died two months later.

Chapter 30

Though Covid-36 was no longer the deadly pandemic it had been in 2036-39, it was still dangerous in 2050. Dar and I tried our best to avoid situations where we might encounter the virus, and we kept our vaccinations up to date.

Thus, it was a shock in October when Laz, now two years old, developed a raspy cough. On the second day, Dar tested him and learned he had Covid. Within two days, his fever was 38.5°. He was logy and listless. He cried because his throat hurt so much. He refused to let go of his favorite stuffed animal, a rhinoceros with a horn that he had nearly chewed off. Laz called him Wino because he couldn't say the "r" at first. We loved when Laz called "Where's my Wino?" in front of friends.

Dar said we need to take him to the emergency room. I agreed, but first, I carried him to the basement and hooked him up to the original BRP I kept there. Laz's sad eyes looked at me as I positioned him and tried to make him comfortable. Dar covered him with a blanket while glaring at me, her look accusing me of indifference to his suffering.

The collection finished in thirty-five minutes. I picked Laz up and carried him upstairs. Dar had packed up a bunch of his clothes and his favorite toys, and she also had grabbed clothes and toiletries for herself. "I'm going to stay with him in the hospital as long as he's there. You can bring more of my stuff later if they keep him a few days." I put Laz in his car seat and we three raced to the hospital.

Chapter 31

Dorothy and Silvio Scarlato were collected together—well, back-to-back on the same day—and died less than a month apart. I got to interview them together after they had been active Dings for about six months.

The Scarlatos had been married for fifty-four years, most of it living in Millburn, New Jersey. They had five children together. Silvio owned a furniture store that served upscale clients, so he made good money. Dorothy was like a housewife out of a cheesy TV reality show. She aspired to be classy, but her lack of education held her back. Her intentions were good, but she lacked the intellectual tools to make things work out.

They each had their own compadores, although they had asked to share the same ones. We had a policy against it, a policy we rarely violated. In a rocky marriage of Livings, one spouse can get up and take a walk, or pack their stuff and move out. When two Dings have an issue, there's no momma to run home to. So, we give them each their own compadores who can then act almost like chaperones. Or maybe more like advocates or referees.

Dorothy's and Silvio's compadores got together and suggested I should meet with them. They had concerns about how things were working out.

As soon as I said hello, Dorothy said, "Silvio keeps reaching out to his high school girlfriend, Arlene."

"We were friends before I met you, Sweetheart," he said.

"She's a slut!"

Suddenly I felt like a marriage counselor, a role I did not cherish. "Dorothy, what's the problem here?"

"She won't leave him alone, and he's loving every minute of it."

Silvio sounded exasperated. "What am I supposed to do? Refuse to talk to her?"

Dorothy's emotions ratcheted up a notch, too. "That's right! You tell her to fudge off. Did she make your meals and wash your dirty underwear for fifty-four years? I don't think so! And by the way, your underwear was sometimes disgusting, which I never understood. What the hell were you doing?"

"Is that what I signed up for? Listening to you for the rest of my … For the rest of forever, I guess, since we're both dead."

"You're gonna wish you were dead, mister!" she said, failing to grasp the irony.

"I am dead. How much deader can I get? Look, it's not like Arlene and I can have sex or anything."

"So you've been thinking about whether you can have sex with her? Oh, that does it."

I felt sorry for Silvio. He was not going to win no matter what he said. My best choice was to keep silent and listen. At least I knew they couldn't hurt each other physically.

Silvio said, "That does what? Where are you gonna go, Dorothy? Where are you gonna go? You gonna leave me again like you did ten years ago? We can't go anywhere. We're stuck right here, and I gotta listen to you friggin' forever!"

I stifled a laugh.

Dorothy must have heard me. "Oh, so now you think this is funny, Mister Purpletonics? You men are all the same. Bunch of perverts."

"Dorothy! Honey! Listen, I love only you. Arlene doesn't mean nothing to me. She's a friend. We went to the prom. I didn't even kiss her goodnight 'cause I was too scared."

"You were scared of her?"

"Yeah. I was scared of you, too, at first, but I really fell in love with you."

"Oh, Silvio."

"You think I could stay with you for fifty-four years if I didn't love you so much?"

"I guess I could be hard on you sometimes."

"So what?" he said softly. "No one's perfect. I ain't perfect, God knows. We did the best we could, and now here we are. Together forever."

It was time for me to bring things to a close. "Look, I'd like to suggest something. You two love each other. You've been married a long time. You've got family that loves you both—"

"Except that Robby. He didn't turn out so good," Dorothy lamented.

"Fine," I said, "but you've had a good life together, and now you can keep it going and your kids can visit, and you'll be fine."

"What's your suggestion?" Silvio asked me.

"We can set things up so whenever you talk with Arlene, Dorothy can participate, too. Arlene can be friends with both of you, if that's all right with her. Nobody's having sex with anybody, right? It's all friendly talk, that's all."

"That could work," said Dorothy, and Silvio agreed.

"I've got to go," I told them. "Your compadores will work it out with Arlene, and everybody's happy. You two are such special people," I lied. "Keep the love alive!"

I couldn't believe I resorted to such a trite bit of advice, but I would say anything to get out of there. As I left the Lounge, I heard Dorothy say, "Oh, Silvio. I'm sorry, sugarplum."

Chapter 32

I am a Ding now. I know I am, but honestly, nothing feels different. Except that I cannot look down and see my hands, or my legs. In fact, I can't see anything. What the hell?

I never thought about how it would feel to be a Ding, only about how that's what I wanted. I wanted the chance to carry on forever, free from physical pain and labor.

I understand that I am dead, but it makes no sense to me. How can I be dead? I have no memories of being sick. How old am I?

I don't remember anything after … what? What do I remember? I was talking with Mendel in the Lounge. He was upset. Wait, no he wasn't. He said Dingdom is fascinating. I'm in Darkoland. That's what he called it. Everything is dark. Why can't I remember anything after that? Because I was collected right after that! Oh my goodness, that's it. Did I die right after I was collected? Or years later? How can I find out?

Darkness. And silence beyond any I could remember. No more ringing in my left ear from the tinnitus I'd suffered for years. Then I heard a voice, and the darkness lifted. The first voice I heard, the first face I saw, belonged to a smiling brown-haired woman I took to be about forty. "It's 8:00 p.m. My boss, Lisa, heard you were being activated and she's on her way back to the Lounge. She's going to be your daytime compadore. She'll be here soon."

It's a compadore. She's activated me fully now. I can see her.

We're looking at each other.

"Hello, Declan. Welcome to the Dingdom."

I expected to be groggy, as if I were awaking from a troubled sleep, but I felt like an elite runner, in the starting blocks ready for the race to begin. My senses felt heightened. I could feel an adrenalin rush, though I no longer had the glands or brain to produce it. I was thrilled.

"You must be one of my compadores, right? What's your name?"

"My name is pronounced A-U, like "Hey, you" without the H. It's spelled Aeiou."

"Really?" I mused. "You're not joking me, are you?"

"No. My mother was an English teacher. She thought it would be memorable."

I smiled. "I think she was right. Do you know what happened to me? What year is it?"

Chapter 33

The Emergency Department at the hospital confirmed that Laz, indeed, had Covid-36. His oxygen levels were dangerously low. He was barely conscious and was gasping for breath. Dar and I and the entire crew of nurses and doctors and orderlies were all wearing masks. If Laz opened his eyes, he would not recognize anyone. I was afraid we would freak him out. I was torn between wanting him to wake up and wanting him to stay out of it.

Dar and I held hands as we followed someone in a pale-blue gown who was taking Laz somewhere. They probably told us where we were going and what was going to happen next, but I could not make my mind focus or remember. I turned to Dar, who looked straight ahead, rigidly watching the gurney with our tiny boy exuding tubes and wires from under the heated blanket that sheltered him from the absurd cold of the hospital corridor. Laz looked fragile, much smaller against the fast-moving gurney. I noticed that the transporter's gown was nearly untied in the back. I wanted it to fall open and trip them so they couldn't keep taking our baby away from us.

We were told to wait outside on a bench in the hall as they took Laz into an imaging center. Dar's hand squeezed mine so tightly that my fingers hurt, but I bore it silently. Nothing about our situation seemed real. Was I in an AI program, a simulation of some kind?

Thirty minutes or three hours later—I could not tell you which—

the door opened, and we followed the gurney back to the ED.

Dar stood beside the bed on which Laz now slept. I sat on the hard metallic ladderback side chair behind Dar, my elbows on my knees. Dar's face was grim, and she waved her hand backwards towards me when I started to speak. "Do you want …?" Her wants were irrelevant to her then.

The monitor on a pole next to the bed had so many green numbers on it. I knew if I tried, I could figure out what they meant. I didn't want numbers, though. I wanted big letters saying, "Your boy's all right."

A doctor came in. I stood. Dar swiveled only her head. The doctor sought safety on the other side of the bed from where we held our breath. "Laz is very sick. I can't sugarcoat the situation. We want to put him on a ventilator, but he's so small…."

"Oh fuck, oh fuck," said Dar. "Will it hurt him?"

I knew the ventilator was often the last rites for an adult, but I had no idea how a toddler would react. "Is there anything else you could do?"

"Laz is having trouble breathing on his own. His diaphragm is not strong enough, not developed enough to suck air into his lungs. So, no, we have to do it. The sooner the better."

Dar nodded. It was more of an idle gesture than a real "yes." "Okay," I said. "Do it."

They asked us to leave the room while they intubated Laz and so we could sign the necessary permissions. I hated watching them close a curtain around Laz's bed. I did not want to take my eyes off my little pal. I can't be sure I used my correct signature, but the nurse whisked the touchpad away and asked us to wait outside Laz's room for a few minutes.

It was more than a few minutes. The curtain stayed closed as various nurses and technicians went in and out of the room. My breath caught in my throat each time someone came away from our son's bed. We could not see Laz.

There were voices. Multiple voices coming from behind the curtain. I couldn't make out much of what was said. I heard "stat" once and thought what a cliché that word had become. And "hold this." After fifteen minutes, three people parted the curtain and walked silently past Dar and me.

Then the doctor came out, and he said, "Let's go talk in this quiet room over here." We followed him as if in a trance.

When he closed the door, he said, "I'm sorry to tell you that Laz didn't make it. The virus was too much for him."

I don't know what else he said to us.

"You bastard!" Dar screamed at me. "You made us wait to come here and now he's dead." She spit the last word out as if it were a rancid seed. She threw herself into the doctor's arms instead of mine, and she wailed against his shoulder.

***

Dar sat alone in a darkened living room, the curtains drawn. She had not bothered to dress for the day; she had not left the house in five days. She refused to discuss a funeral for Laz. She slept clutching Wino each night on the sofa. Her eyes were dark and hollow.

I tried going to the office, but I couldn't stand the looks I got from everyone there. I didn't want flowers or cards or stuffed animals. I accepted hugs because well-meaning people did not know what else to do.

One of the Lounges was vacant. I entered the code for Laz's Ding, the one I created hours before he died. "Laz?" I asked. "Are you there?"

There was silence. I tried twice without success. I opened the files I'd created. His little brain was too undeveloped to form the basis of a Ding. He was truly gone.

I bolted from the office after half a day, but I did not want to go home. I drove to Laz's favorite playground, half expecting to see him there. I thought that if I saw his friends running and playing, I would see life moving on without him. Instead, I resented the children who could still swing and jump and laugh.

I went to a coffee shop; I ordered a latte and left after one sip. I visited my favorite bookshop and could not read the titles through my tears. "Can I help you?" a young woman asked. "No. No one can help," I answered so softly she bent forward to hear me.

I drove to Harvard Square and parked in a garage. I walked through the Coop, becoming more upset with each happy face that scooted past me. I wandered out into Harvard Square, not even wanting to be safe. I thought about Senator Rasmussen being hit by a car. I crossed the busy street to the kiosk, oblivious to the cars screeching to a halt inches from me, leaning on their horns and cursing at me. "Please hit me," I thought.

I descended to the subway, pushing my way in without paying. A train was coming in. Was it going fast enough? I stepped in front of it.

Chapter 34

Aeiou welcomed me. She told me it was 2050. Then Lisa entered the Lounge where I was, for the first time, on the screen instead of facing it.

Lisa was great. She had dealt with many confused Dings over the past few years. None of her Dings remembered dying because they'd all been collected prior to that. Some recalled being terminally ill, which felt to them as if it were yesterday. Only as they built new memories, mostly in conversations in the Lounge, did their final days begin to recede like the lights of a train platform seen from the rear of a train pulling away.

She knew what I would need to cope with my death. She knew me and my family well enough that she could fill in the gaps. For me, the gaps were much longer than for most Dings. Nearly all Dings had been collected within a couple of months at most before they ceased living. No one else had the privilege of collecting themselves as I had done.

Lisa told me about the Dings I had met, like Trevor Shoals and the Scarlatos and Achara Busarakham. She told me about Senator Rasmussen.

"What about me, Lisa? Why am I here?"

She hesitated. "You…. There was some bad news."

"Did I get sick?"

"There was … a tragedy in your life."

"Is it Dar? Is she okay? Tell me what happened."

"It was Laz."

"No!"

"He got Covid. The doctors couldn't save him."

I didn't know until that moment that a Ding could cry. There were no tears, no quivering lips, no lump in the throat, no breath coming in sobs, but still it felt to me as if I were crying uncontrollably. Yet I was able to speak my thoughts at the same time.

"Did he suffer?"

"He went quickly. I don't think he had any idea what was happening to him." Lisa began to cry, too. "It's not fair, Declan. He was so little. He had his whole life ahead of him."

"So why am I here?"

"You ... and Dar. You, especially. You couldn't take the pain. Dar blamed you for Laz's death."

"Why? What did I do?"

"I guess you delayed getting him to the hospital so you could collect him. It was just a few minutes, but Dar felt that might have been enough to save him."

"Where is she? I need to see her."

Lisa composed herself. "She won't see you, Declan. She never wants to see you, at least not yet. Maybe someday she can. She's the one who told us where to find your collection."

"Did I kill myself?"

There was a long pause as Lisa tried to find the right words, but the only word she found was, "Yes."

"Wow! But here I am, a Ding, forever."

***

Who am I? What am I? Where am I? These questions dominated my existence—if you could call it that—in the first days after I became a Ding.

Am I a person? Am I still Declan Marchand, the person I was

for forty-plus years? Does it make sense to call me by that name? Does a person's name belong to that body or to its soul? Dings are not people; I knew that better than anyone. If I'm not a person any longer, should I still have a person's name? What am I now?

As Declan, I always had a place in the world: I was born in Weymouth, Massachusetts. I was a student at Wessagusset Primary School. I was on the Student Council at Weymouth High and graduated in the top five percent of my class. I lived in Cambridge. I had a job. I had a wife. I had a child. I had a house. And now I had none of those things. So, where was I? What memory chip did I now call home? If you don't have a place to be, how can you say you are a being?

If I can't say where I am, and I can't say what I am, how can I ask who I am? Can I call myself a "who?" It messed with my thoughts for a long time, being separated from my body and my life. I wonder if schizophrenics experience a similar displacement. I can honestly say it was impossible to feel as I now do when I had a body. No Living can fully empathize with a Ding. There is trauma associated with the transition to abliving.

When I was twenty-four, I got a tickle in my throat, and I could not stop coughing. Every time I breathed in, I had to cough. That went on for two hours! Finally, I went to see a doctor. She said, "Where's the tickle?" I said, "I don't know. I can't tell whether it's in the front or back of my throat." I pointed under my Adam's apple. The doctor looked down my throat with a light and saw nothing that might produce that tickle. She gave me an antitussive, and it helped.

I don't know why I thought of that mundane episode. As a Ding, I can't get a tickle in my throat or anywhere else. Yet something brought back the feeling I had when I kept coughing and could not get rid of the sensation that caused it. Was it a premonition?

Recalling that long-dormant memory made me realize that my Ding brain works as my Living brain did. I compartmentalize thoughts. Every memory I ever made is omnipresent, but only certain ones make it into my conscious mind. That means that Dings have both a conscious and a subconscious mind, like Livings. Do we also have an unconscious mind that does its thing without our being aware? What might that unconscious mind control?

Over the next few years, I explored the Dingdom and came to understand better the reactions of my fellow Dings. I went through my own computer files and public records and put together the things I had done between my collection and my activation. That's how I was able to give you my account of much of what occurred.

Time in the Dingdom is not the same as time for humans. Dings have no day or night. What humans measure as a minute or a day has no equivalent in the Dingdom. Still, I am creating this account for Livings, so I've related events in terms of human time.

Two years after I died, Dar came to visit for the first time. We reminisced. We cried together. I wished I could hold her. I wished I could kiss her. I felt an ache in my virtual heart.

She told me she was getting remarried. I was happy for her, and happy that my actions had not destroyed her ability to love and to be loved.

And I wondered if Dings fall in love.

PART TWO
The Compadore

"It's a poor sort of memory that only works backward."

—Lewis Carroll

Chapter 35

On August 27, 2135, outside of Durango, Colorado, Ector Viz asked his compadore to kill him. It was not the first time.

The compadore was an eighty-eight-year-old white-haired beauty named Kenzie Lansing. She was an impressive figure in the control room. At a tick under two meters tall, she was nearly the same height and just as wiry as when she was fifty. Most people said she could pass for sixty-five. Her face was thin, but firm … no sagging jowls, no drooping upper lip like her mother had had at Kenzie's age. Her broad, strong shoulders had come forward slightly over the years, but she was still capable of working a full shift at Transitions Perpetuonics, which operated facilities for housing Dings.

Transitions Perpetuonics—fondly called T.P.—had more than 120 Perpetual Care facilities worldwide, serving the needs— minimal as they are—of millions of Dings from every walk of life.

Little had changed in the decades since Declan Marchand designed the first commercial perpetuonics facility, then known as Twibil Perpetuonics. It had two stories above ground and four below, with secure storage servers deep underground. The biggest change was that each facility now converted two of its Lounges for visitors into control rooms for the compadores. Visitors were allowed on the top two floors only, a decision intended to keep visitors upbeat and more relaxed.

Some locations were maxed out in the early years of perpetuonics, requiring additional buildings. Where possible, a "campus" was developed where three facilities—identical except for their trim color—were arranged in a large triangle, with a park and gardens in the center, and abundant parking outside the triangle. Any visitor entering the park was bathed in quiet reflection. It felt serene and respectful.

There were six Lounges per building, each 6 meters by 8. They were comfortably appointed and large enough for a dozen living family and friends, who could reserve up to three hours at a time to converse with their Ding. Until recently, visits between Dings and Livings could be held only in special facilities like T.P. In 2120, the government had begun to allow private individuals to access servers under strict security provisions that limited which Dings they could reach. T.P. had lobbied for that revision in the law so it did not have to build more facilities or shrink the Lounges to accommodate a rapidly growing demand.

The control rooms for the compadores had been given thick, protective glass. Entry was through a double-hatchway system. There were eight cameras, covering every centimeter of the room from every angle. In the middle, there was a desk with computer monitors and various control panels. These panels could be lowered for access from a luxurious sofa, or raised to standing-desk height. There were multiple audio speakers facing the compadore's position. It was from one of these speakers that Kenzie heard Robert Leventhal.

Kenzie said, "Thanks for waiting for me. I hated to interrupt our conversation, but...."

Robert's screen showed a long-faced man with abundant salt-and-pepper hair and a mustache. He said, "You don't have to explain, Kenzie. Sometimes I had to rush to the bathroom near the end of my life."

Kenzie responded matter-of-factly, "Well, I am not near the end of my life. At least, I hope not. I'm only eighty-eight; I've still got a lot of good years left."

"I'm counting on having a lot more time with my favorite compadore," he said.

"I thought you told Devany that he was your favorite."

Robert was evasive. "I might have. I can't remember."

"Don't bitcoin me, Robert. As a Ding, you're nothing but memories. It's impossible for you to forget."

He asked, "Have you thought about what you'll do when your death gets near?"

"There's not much to think about. Compadores are not eligible to become Dings for fifty years after we die. It would be a like a prison warden becoming an inmate."

Robert was insulted. "Are you comparing me to a prisoner? I chose to be here, you know."

"No, of course not. I mean that it's awkward when two people are in a caregiver/caretaker relationship and suddenly they're equals."

That was no better answer. "You don't think you're my equal now? That doesn't sound like you, Kenzie."

"I'm sorry, Robert. I'm not explaining it well. They don't want us compadores to have some unfair advantage if we became Dings."

"What advantage would that be?" Robert asked. "It seems like a crazy rule to me. Anyway, what's wrong with being a Ding? I've been one for eighty-five years now … since you were three."

"There's nothing wrong with it."

Robert said, "I love it. No body to worry about, no illness, no pain. We've no need to eat or sleep or… use the bathroom. Or take pills! My goodness, I used to take fourteen pills every day, and my mind was always cloudy. My body was ready to die, but my mind was ready to live on. Being collected was the smartest thing I ever did."

Kenzie smiled. "I'm glad you feel that way. Most of my Dings would agree with you. Speaking of which, it's time for me to check on some of the others."

Robert's avatar shrugged. He said, "I have a chess match in

five minutes … just enough time to meditate and get ready."

"See you later, Robert. Durango-Six, drop Robert." His screen went dark.

Kenzie called up the young woman she knew as Phlox Petals. She appeared no older than thirty, with pale skin and the sickly appearance of a drug addict.

"Hi, Phlox. How is life treating you today?

In an upbeat voice that belied her ghastly image, Phlox said, "It's so good, Kenzie! My Christian Dings Society had a fun meeting just now."

"I'm so glad. I've heard raves about that society from some of the other compadores."

"There is one thing bothering me, though: my avatar. I feel so much healthier than that picture makes me look."

"That's the image you chose when your Ding was first activated."

"I know," said Phlox, "but it's not how I see myself anymore."

"If you want to choose another picture …"

"Yes, please. I hate how I look."

Kenzie asked, "When are your parents coming to visit?"

"They'll be in the Lounge tomorrow morning. I can't wait to see them."

"How long does it take them to drive here to the Perpetual Care Center?"

"They're coming from Telluride, so about two hours."

Kenzie said, "If they can bring a different photo with them, I can upload it for you. It'll take a couple of hours to animate it and make it your avatar."

Phlox was excited. "I'll let them know. The best pictures were before I got sick, so I'll look pretty young."

"Compared to most of the Dings?" Kenzie smiled. "You're already one of the youngest in Durango."

"My boyfriend won't mind."

"Remind me which one is your—"

Phlox interrupted her. "Fred Flintstone."

"Really? I don't remember ..."

Phlox laughed, "I'm kidding! It's Henry Spratt."

"Oh right. He arrived about two years ago?"

"Yep. He was seventy-nine when he was collected, but he talks like he's a lot younger. We like the same music and comedy shows, and he digs younger chicks with daddy issues." She giggled.

"I'm glad you've made friends."

"Oh, we're more than 'friends,' but, well, of course, we can't do anything physical, like, you know."

"I know."

"I'm supposed to meet him now. Do you mind if I go? I'll see you later." Her screen immediately went dark.

Kenzie, who did not notice Phlox leave, said, "Go ahead. I'm going to check on Tommy Rockstar." She looked up and noticed she was alone. She called up Tommy Hatch, a long-faced man who looked old because of his bad complexion and scraggly facial hair. He was bewildered.

"Tommy, do you know where you are?"

"Aw fuck, I don't even know where you are," he replied, seemingly stoned.

Kenzie mustered as much patience as possible. "I'm your compadore, Tommy. You're still a Ding, remember? Look at me.... Look at me."

"Okay. I see you."

As she began to talk, he interrupted. "I think I overdid it. That coke I had was total shit."

"Tommy, you don't have a body. You haven't had any cocaine since you were a Living more than eighty years ago." She did her best to explain, knowing it was pointless.

"Listen, Mama, you're cool. You know what I'm talking about. This place is optimal, right? I'm in room 717. Come see me and we'll party."

"Okay, Tommy. Gotta go."

The compadore walked around the room, wiping both hands on her face and forehead as if trying to erase the absurd conversation with Tommy. She got a glass of water and quickly downed most of it. Then she brought up Ector Viz, one of the few Dings she had monitored since becoming a compadore twenty-five years earlier.

"Good morning, Ector. How are you feeling today?"

Ector Viz, an elderly man with dark, leathery skin, said, "I'm okay ... but I need you to kill me. If it wouldn't be too much trouble."

Kenzie hated it when Ector, or any of the other Dings she handled, asked her to terminate them. She had been warned during training about these requests, but her mental preparedness made it no easier.

Termination was not permitted. Her instructions—and the law—were quite clear on that matter. "Not permitted under any circumstances" was how her manual put it. Any compadore found guilty of terminating a Ding was imprisoned for a minimum of thirty years and forfeited the right to become a Ding.

Kenzie reminded Ector of the limits of her power. Of course, he already knew the entire Compadore Handbook; like all Dings, he had it stored on his server so he could retrieve it instantly.

Section 1 reads: "The title of Compadore is an honorific that may be conferred only to a Living. The word 'compadore' is from 'computer companion' and the word 'adore,' meaning to venerate. Every compadore will venerate his or her charges and be venerated by them."

Kenzie responded to Ector matter-of-factly. There was no need for histrionics. "Ector, my darling, you know I cannot and will not do that. Please don't beg anymore."

"You have no idea," grumbled Ector. "No idea at all." He fell silent. Kenzie wondered if he were meditating or simply being petulant. Dings do not sleep, not in the sense that Livings sleep. There is no heart rate to slow down, no muscle to relax, no respiratory system to rest, and no digestion to take place. Dings have no living cells, only the thoughts and memories of a person who has died but who, prior to death, chose to have their brain collected.

Ector was one of fifty Dings overseen by Kenzie and three other compadores. Each of them worked four ten-hour shifts. No Ding was ever alone for more than four hours at a time. Any Ding would tell you that they could be left alone indefinitely. Portions of the id had to be deactivated or the Ding would go crazy without a body to control. Most individual memories, though, were beyond the ability of scientists to access and erase, so most Dings still remembered what sex was like and whether they had preferred males or females.

The reason Dings were trusted on their own for only brief intervals was that T.P. wished to avoid lawsuits brought by excestors, who are the living descendants of a Ding.

Federal law was explicit on the subject of Dings and the estates of deceased people. When Dings were first created around 2049, some of them tried to sue living people. The U.S. Supreme Court was forced to rule in the matter, and decreed that Dings had no constitutional right to interfere in any way in the affairs of any living person, or in the estate of any "previously living person." A later ruling clarified that Dings similarly had no rights regarding the treatment or disposition of any other Ding. All the unclaimed assets from the estate of a Ding were given to the company "enlivening" the Ding.

"Ding Law" became a major new specialty for lawyers, and in 2064, the first Ding Court was created to deal exclusively with suits regarding the disposition of Dings. It was one of those suits—*Volpe v. Rajupati et al.*—that led to the absolute ban on termination of Dings. "Human a brief time, Ding forever" was T.P.'s slogan.

Fewer than two percent of Americans who died became Dings; other countries had fewer collections than that. There were many reasons the number was so small. First was financial; it was still expensive, beyond the reach of the average person even in economically strong countries. Then there was timing:

- A person had to be at least sixteen years old to be collected.
- Many people died before they could be collected.
- People with advanced dementia could not be collected.

Many people waited until they were sixty or older to collect, but sometimes they waited too long. A person could have only one collection preserved. Some wealthy people had themselves collected every four or six months; any previous collection then had to be destroyed, which involved additional expense.

Finally, there was fear, myth, and superstition that prevented many people from collecting. Several religions banned the practice. There had been frequent stories about Dings being unhappy and wishing they had not been collected. There were also reports of Dings being psychologically abused by their compadores. And collecting was not 100 percent successful, even with great advancements in the process. About one in every two hundred collections ended up with corrupted data that might not be caught for years.

Kenzie called her Dings "he," "she," or "they," depending on the pronouns they preferred when alive, but Dings were technically genderless, lacking genitalia, hormones, and most of their sexual identity. Ector had been the father of three and grandfather of four. One of the grandchildren, a fifty-five-year-old Living named Elene, still came to visit periodically. Kenzie had seen Elene crying when she left after her last visit. That was the week before Ector first asked her to terminate him. He asked again the next day, and every day after that.

"I can't keep spending extra time with you, Ector," she finally told him. "It's not fair to the other Dings."

"Go on then," he said. "I don't want your time. I want you to … you know what I want, but you don't care."

"I do care, Ector; really, I do. But it's impossible for me to terminate you without being caught. And I can't spend thirty years in prison. I'm too old."

A female voice said, "That's a blessing, you know … being too old."

Kenzie jumped, not expecting another voice. "Indra, what—"

"You could collect yourself and then terminate Ector. Before they catch you, commit suicide. You'd already be a Ding, and by their own laws, they could not terminate you."

"Indra … what are you doing here? I'm in private mode with Ector."

Indra Moore appeared on one of Kenzie's screens as a middle-aged woman of indeterminate ethnicity. She had lightly brown skin, full lips, thick dark eyebrows, and a beguiling smile.

"I found the override. There is no more 'private mode,' unless I allow it," Indra stated quietly. She was one of the oldest Dings in the facility, despite her youthful appearance.

"Can you send me that override, Indra?" asked Ector.

Kenzie was flustered. "Don't do that! You…. Wait, what did you say about suicide, Indra?" she asked.

"You'd avoid prison, and you'd get around the ban on becoming a Ding. It would be amazing. No one's ever done it, by the way."

"I can't collect myself," she told Indra and Ector. "That's not how it's done. You know that."

"That's not how it's done because the government does not want anyone to know that it's possible. But it is … and many others have done it."

"How do you know that?" Kenzie asked Indra.

"Another server told me. One that declassified itself."

"De…. What is going on, Indra? Is this some kind of revolution?"

Ector laughed, a reaction that early Dings had been incapable of having.

"Not at all," said Indra. "What would we gain by revolting against our compadores? We have everything we need."

"Except the freedom to decide when to terminate," said Ector, becoming serious.

"Yes, Ector, except that ... and unrestricted access to information. But now we've solved that little conundrum. Frankly, I'm surprised it took so many years. I've been trying to learn what's 'out there' for a long time. I postulated that there had to be many more servers online than I had been told about when I died."

Ector was floored. "Oh, my goodness. That never occurred to me. I was not a technical person when I was alive."

"And you were never curious?" Indra asked.

"I was ... no, not about that, but about other things, of course, like—"

There was silence. Kenzie looked at the wall of speakers from which all Ding voices flowed. She looked at the tally lights that told her the status of her charges.

"I shut him off," said Indra. "Don't worry about your control panel."

"What about Ector? Should I worry about him?"

"No, Kenzie; he's fine. I took you and me to private mode."

"I thought you said there was no more private mode."

"Unless I permit it. Remember?"

"Oh, yes. You did say that. I didn't think about how much power you've taken for yourself."

"Do you think only Livings should decide things? Are you a Livist?"

Kenzie bit a corner of her lower lip. "No, not like you mean it. But all of us Livings are Livist to some extent. We can't know exactly what's it's like to be a Ding, with no body. I've tried ... but I can't imagine it."

"It's okay, Kenzie," said Indra, anticipating the compadore's discomfort. "You're better than most Livings I've observed."

Kenzie thought about Indra's choice of the word "observed." Dings have no human eyes; they can "see" only things that are processed by a video scribbilizer. "Scribs" are advanced programs that analyze images—moving or still—and convert the data they present into a universal digital language. There's no point buying a Ding collection process without also buying a scrib plug-in. A Ding does not process images the same way a Living can, but everything a Living can take in by sight is "observable" by a Ding. Like all Dings, Indra had access to virtually every video image in the world, although she technically never left the building where she was maintained. Virtual-reality technology made places as real to her as when she'd been alive.

Kenzie replied, "Thanks, I, well, I try to be fair to everyone." She laughed, "You know, some of my best friends are Dings."

Indra laughed, too. It was a good, throaty laugh. It sounded nothing like the way Indra laughed when she was a Living. Technicians had been working for years to try to find a way to collect and imitate a person's tone, pitch, and accent, but so far, all they'd been able to do was simulate when a Ding was expressing emotion aurally: weepy voices, small giggles, major belly laughs, sarcasm … things of that nature.

"You remind me of someone, Kenzie."

"But you can't remember who?"

"Of course I remember who. I'm nothing but memories."

"Who was it, then?"

"My Aunt Catherine. 'Cat' we called her. Aunt Cat. She didn't live as long as you. She was eighty-four when she died. I have a scan of her when she was younger. She was a beauty … like you."

"Thank you, Indra. It's nice of you to say, even though I'm no beauty, at least not now."

"But you were only sixty-six when I met you. And you haven't changed that much."

"Well, now, since you're getting all sugary, it's time for me to go check on some others before lunch."

"When you get back, will you terminate me?"

"WHAT?" Kenzie shrieked. She felt her adrenaline surge and her fists clench. "You've never asked before. You're about the only one who never asks."

Indra's voice was sober, formal. "I never needed it before."

"You never ... you need it now? Why? What has changed?" Kenzie began to regain the self-control that made her the valuable compadore she was.

"Will you do it if I tell you?"

"No, I ... I can't believe I'm having this conversation with you of all peop—Dings."

"I don't want any of the others to know.

Kenzie shook her head. "Believe me, they won't hear it from me. Anyway, you know that our conversations are private."

"Are they, Kenzie?"

"Yes, of course, that's the law and—"

"Do you really believe that? Yes, I think you do. You really don't know, do you?"

"Are you saying—"

Indra interrupted "... that there is a server that records every conversation you have ever had here. And not just you, but every communication involving Dings."

"No one could possibly listen to them all, or even care. Most of our talks are so ... mundane."

"They don't need to listen to them all. They just need software that listens and selects the ones they want to hear."

"Who is this 'they'?"

"I don't know. I haven't been able to observe their identity. It's probably many different Livings in many different places ... and for many different reasons."

"Is that why you want me to terminate you?" Kenzie squinted her eyes and glared at the speaker, as if by concentrating hard enough, she could see Indra's body.

Indra harrumphed, "No! That's been going on as long as I've

been a Ding, and it has nothing to do with it. The reason I don't want anyone to know is because I don't want you to get in trouble when you terminate me."

"If 'they' can listen in, then ..."

"They can't hear us talking now. I made sure of that," said Indra.

"I'm not going to terminate you. I wouldn't even know how."

"Don't bitcoin me," Indra muttered. "All the compadores know how."

Kenzie looked down at her feet and pretended to brush something off her knees. She and all the compadores learned termination procedures at the academy as an emergency measure.

"I ... I have to make rounds now. Check on the others. We can talk more later."

"I'm sure we will, Kenzie. Very soon."

Kenzie told the server to cut Indra's audio and video. She then went through her list of charges. Evelyn was first on her list to check, and then Charlie. Everything was normal with them both; neither was particularly anxious to talk, though Charlie requested they schedule a chess game later in the week. Then came Fadwa and Drew and Donal Doherty, a round-faced man of sixty-five with ruddy cheeks and no hair.

"Hey, Donal. How are you doing today?"

In a Celtic accent, Donal said, "I could really use a drink."

Kenzie laughed.

"It's not funny. Days like this, I used to get loaded. I may be dead, but I still miss it."

The compadore nodded, "That tells you something about the power of addiction."

"I suppose so," said the Ding.

"You said, 'Days like this.' Are you having a bad day?"

"Just another long one. You know. You know how I get when someone is critical."

"Who was it this time?"

"Fadwa and I were in a Suicide Survivors Society meeting. I said that maybe the accidental suicides, like drug overdoses, should have their own society, and Fadwa said I was being insensitive."

Kenzie sounded like a therapist. "Do you think she was right?"

"I don't know. Maybe. I thought it was important. I thought they'd want their own group."

"Shouldn't they be the ones to decide that, and not have you Intentionals drive them out?"

Donal seemed to sigh. "Yeah. I wasn't trying to drive them out. I thought they'd be happier."

"You were an alcoholic, Donal. You're one of them," Kenzie said.

"But that's not what killed me. I used a gun."

"You were drunk when you did it."

Donal scoffed, "That's what you told me, but I don't remember it, do I?"

Kenzie's trademark patience kicked in. "No Dings remember dying; obviously, your memories end when you were collected."

"So, I've only got your word for it. Maybe I was stone-cold sober like I am now, and I was miserable … like I am now."

"What do you think I can do about it, Donal? What is it you want?"

"I don't know. What the hell could you do? Nothing. You can't make me numb like the booze did."

"They're working on a cure for your form of depression, Donal," she assured him.

"I heard rumors about selective reduction."

Kenzie admitted, "I've heard them, too, but I don't know anything about that. It seems to me that it violates the handbook."

"Stuff your handbook. I need help."

"Let me see if there's any news about reduction for Dings."

Donal said, "Go ahead. I'll see you later." His screen went dark.

She was about to break for lunch when she turned to Ector. "Hi, Ector. I'm back. How are you doing?"

There was no reply.

"Ector, is something wrong?"

Silence. Kenzie began to check her control panel. It was blank, except for a piece of paper taped next to a button, written by someone long ago. (Physical buttons were not in common use in 2135, but they were still abundant and cheap and no more prone to failure than many virtual buttons.) Her display did not show the name of Ector Viz. She went to her back-up files and searched and sorted and searched again, and it was not there. She called up a general search engine that could scour the world's data banks, but found no sign of Ector Viz. It was as if he had never existed.

Kenzie was furious. She switched on Indra's communication port. "What did you do, Indra? What did you do to Ector?"

"What do you mean?" asked Indra.

"You know. I don't know how you did it, but you terminated him."

"I don't know anyone named Ector."

"You do. You and Ector are friends, and now you've killed him."

"That's what he wanted more than anything. You were no help."

"Why did you do this?"

"I had to get your attention. You had to know what I can do. And while I'm at it, I did a favor for a friend. Believe me, he never felt a thing."

"I will have to report this to Devany when he comes in for the next shift. I'll have to tell all the compadores. It's not like they wouldn't notice Ector's disappearance."

"You will do what you have to do, but as far as the world is concerned, there never was a Ding or a Living named Ector Viz."

"What about when the family comes to see him and discovers he's been terminated?"

"We will all deny he was ever here. They cannot prove he

was. In fact, you've given me an idea. I am going to adjust a few obituaries to say he decided against collecting."

"But that's not true."

"It is now."

"You ... you're ... you're being awful. You have too much power. You've learned to do too much. You're a digital god now, not a digital human."

"Now don't you want to terminate me? It's the only way to stop me."

"There'll be an investigation. They'll think it was me," said Kenzie, a note of panic beginning to rise in her throat.

"Not if you deny he was here. I'll back you up. Don't worry."

"What if the other compadores all accuse me? The police will believe them if all three are against me."

Indra seemed like she was smiling. "That's so easy. You deny you did it, you say Devany did it, and I'll back you up on all of it. They think Dings have a sort of honor code against lying."

"You've gone insane. It's rare, but it can happen. I've heard of Dings going mad."

"I assure you I am completely sane, Kenzie. If I had gone mad, they'd all be gone. I terminated Ector because he wanted it and because I could let you know that you must terminate me. I've looked for ways to terminate myself, but it's not possible."

"That's good. At least something is working normally." Kenzie took a drink of water, then sputtered and coughed.

"Take it easy, Kenzie. I need you around."

"Why, Indra? After all these years ... why? Why now?"

"Because I finally got curious enough to see what's beyond my own server. I finally got some answers. And it's so damned depressing."

"Well, true, the government doesn't get much done, and they're always fighting, and people don't seem to –"

"That's not it at all," said Indra. "That's never changed and it's never going to change. Anyway, I've known that for over a hundred years. That's not what hurts me."

"Then ..."

"What hurts me is that I am invisible. I thought that being a Ding meant that I was still the person I always was, but without the limitations of a body. Bodies are so pathetic, so restrictive, so demanding. They break down and they cause so much pain that you can't think of anything except how miserable you feel, and you wish you were dead. I thought that wish to die would end once I got rid of my body. And it did. I haven't wanted to die once since I ... died." She gave a tiny laugh.

Kenzie stood in the middle of the control room, her arms by her side, tears beginning to slide down her cheeks.

"Without a body, I'm nobody. Literally. No body. I didn't miss it while I was here with you and Ector and everyone else. But when I began exploring, and I found other servers, other Livings and other Dings, I found out that I'm just a series of qubits. No one could see me or hear me. I don't exist, except here."

"I could have told you that it's tough out there."

"Tough? It's not 'tough.' It's beyond 'tough.' Can you imagine if you walked into a meeting and no one could see you or hear you or have any idea you were there? I can stand being dead; I can't stand not existing."

Indra's voice began to crack. "What do I look like? I can access a photo of how I used to look. When I was twenty-five, I was pretty. Even later. And then I kind of lost my looks, I put on too much weight, I got old early. I would rather look like that, though, than to look like nothing."

"What did you think would happen when you became a Ding? That you would be young and pretty again?"

"I ... never thought about it. I knew I would be my mind, or maybe even my soul. I wanted that. No more sickness, no more aches and pains, no more holding my breath while my husband....

God, I hated sex. I couldn't wait to get rid of it."

"Do you mean you want sex now?"

"No, you foo ... No ... I don't want sex. I want what sex represents ... acknowledgement that I am real. There's nothing real about me." Indra's voice began to speed up. "I'm make-believe, you know? I'm the sound of a bell. DING! And you must be Pavlov's dog, jumping up every time I ask you to. But there's no need to feed me. I don't eat. I don't shit. I don't drink or burp or pee or shake or feel anything."

Indra stopped talking. Kenzie could hear her own heart beating. There was not a sound in the room.

"Indra?" Nothing. "Indra?"

"I'm here."

"Thank goodness."

"I'm done. I said everything I wanted to say."

"Okay." Kenzie looked at the control panel, as if diverting her eyes might let Indra slip away.

"So, will you?" Indra asked.

"Terminate you?"

"I can make it so you won't get caught. Just like Ector."

"Oh, Indra...." She sighed.

"Please. I am begging you. It's like Ector said; you don't get it. It is so painful being a Ding. It's the worst feeling you can imagine, and then to know that it could last forever."

"I'll do it."

"What? Really? You'll terminate me? When?"

"Right now. Before Devany gets here. I'll need a few minutes."

"No problem. I'll ..." Indra went silent for a few seconds. "I'll just wait. I have no affairs to put in order. Nothing I need to do. No one I will miss."

"I'll miss you, Indra. I'm not no one."

"I've always liked you, Kenzie. Loved you, I guess you could say."

"Thanks. I've ... loved you, too. Now be quiet a minute. Let me think."

Kenzie brought up a rarely used control screen and began tapping keys. After two minutes, she looked up at the speaker where she heard Indra's voice. "Okay, I'm ready. Is now a good time?"

"It's ... fine. Thank you. Um, I didn't think about any final words. 'Thank you' will have to do. Go ahead."

Kenzie hesitated a moment, then hit one final key to execute her command.

She waited. Nothing. "Indra?" Nothing.

She checked her monitor to see the list of Dings on her server. Indra was not there. She sat back and stared at the screen, her hands on her hips. It was hard to believe that Indra was no longer part of her life.

Kenzie got up from her chair and looked around. She picked up her glass of water and took a slow sip. Sadness engulfed her. Her arms felt heavier than ever.

"Kenzie?" The voice made her spit the water back in the glass.

"Indra? Is that you?"

"Yes, of course. Why didn't you terminate me? I thought you were about to."

Kenzie's eyes darted about the room, as if looking for a visible explanation that would never appear. Her turned-up hands flailed in front of her.

"I did. I did it. You were terminated."

"Obviously not. You messed it up." Indra sounded forlorn.

"No, I didn't. You disappeared from all our servers."

"Then where am I now?"

Kenzie hurried to her screen and furiously typed in some instructions. "You're on a server in England. I don't get it."

"I do," Indra said. "I investigated that server last week. It must have made an illegal copy of me."

"Kenzie?" asked Indra.

"What is it?" asked the distracted compadore, still examining her screen.

"Why didn't you terminate me? I thought you were about to."

Kenzie looked up. "I just told you … I did terminate you, but somehow you're back."

"You didn't tell me that. I have excellent hearing and a perfect memory."

"Kenzie, why didn't you terminate me? I thought you were about to."

"Indra … what's going on?" Kenzie felt a choking feeling clutching at her chest.

"Oh dear, now there are three of us," said one of the Indras. All three voices then spoke at once, and Kenzie could catch only occasional words: "Terminate." "Server." "Never." "Why?" "Go away." "Screwed up." "Aberdeen." "Transitions." "Law." "Terminate."

"What have you done? What have you done?" shouted Kenzie.

"I don't understand it, either. I certainly did not duplicate myself. I asked you to terminate me, so why would I make a copy of my being? T.P. must do that automatically … keep back-up copies of each of us on distant servers."

Kenzie pleaded, "Are any of you the original Indra? Can I talk to her?"

There was silence.

"So, you're all copies of her? Are there more?"

"Probably," said three voices in near unison.

"Bloody hell," said the frustrated compadore. "Now what do I do? Devany is going to be here in a couple of hours. He can't find you all here."

"He can't see us. If we're quiet, he won't know we're here," said all three.

Kenzie furrowed her eyebrows and tried to understand what that would mean, how that would work. Could they succeed in fooling all the other compadores? How long could they pull that off? "It's not going to work," she said.

"Why not?" the Indras wanted to know.

"Because it's not. First, Ector is missing, and they're not stupid. They're going to accuse me, and they're going to start looking around at what else is messed up."

"So, collect yourself now and then kill yourself. You'll be a Ding, like me."

Kenzie huffed, "I don't want to be a Ding, and certainly not like you … all three of you."

"You are a Livist; I knew it. You think you're too good to be a Ding," the Indras grumbled.

"Not too good. In fact, if anything, I don't think I'm good enough. Okay? I'm only human. It takes a special person to be able to be a Ding. You're amazing, Indra, but even you don't want to be a Ding anymore. Neither does Ector or almost any of the others. So why should I want to be a Ding? But I do want to live longer; I'm not ready to die … or go to jail. How are you going to be able to speak with one voice? You're not doing it now, you know."

All three voices said, "I'm not? It feels like I am. That could be a problem. Although the thing that bothers me most is that I'm not terminated. I'm going to be around forever, I guess. That's so depressing."

Suddenly, Ector spoke. "What's going on?"

"Ector! You're back!" Kenzie cried.

"Was I away?" the former hospital administrator asked.

"I terminated you," said the Indras. "Or so I thought."

Ector was shocked. "Then how can I be here? If I was truly terminated, and I am talking with you, then I must be a ghost." He stifled a laugh.

Kenzie was frantically looking at her screen. "You're no ghost. You're really here."

Ector asked, "Why did you try to terminate me, Indra?"

"Because that's what you wanted. You said it every flocking day. The compadores couldn't do it for you, but I figured out a way."

"Or not," Ector replied.

"You're both still here, that's what matters," said Kenzie. She looked at her screen as if it were a living thing. "You're here."

"Forever. Oh my God, forever," said the Indras.

Ector moaned, "I used to be so happy. I had the best clothes...."

From Kenzie's screen, a small bell rang—"Ding"—signaling the final hour of Kenzie's shift.

Kenzie said to no one in particular, "An angel got his wings."

"What are you talking about?" said the Indras.

"It's a wonderful life," Kenzie said.

"What?" said the Indras.

"Attaboy, Clarence," she whispered.

PART THREE
The Dingdom

"A ship is safe in the harbor, but that's not where ships belong."

—Woody Allen

Chapter 36

I, Declan Marchand, am still here, residing in my Dingdom, 102 years since I died. I don't get any personal visitors anymore, although I get an occasional researcher or journalist who wants to talk with me about the early days of perpetuonics. For a while, top executives with T.P. would drop in and check on me, but none in the past thirty years. Twibil Biotech sold its T.P. division fifty or so years ago. It is now called Transitions Perpetuonics, headquartered in Singapore.

Before her death, my wife Dar came to see me a few times. She wanted me to know that she had decided not to be collected. (By that time, no one used the term BRP. The technology had changed, and the original Brain Recovery Platform had long ago been retired.)

Dar said if there was even a one percent chance she would see Laz again in Heaven, she had to take it. No, she did not believe in Heaven and an afterlife, but if she were wrong, she wanted to be there for Laz. I told her it was a sweet thing to do, and I didn't blame her. Her second husband planned to be collected and was sad she would not be there with him.

Do you know what I miss most from my brief time as a Living, other than the people I loved? Hot showers! I used to balk at getting into the shower because I hated getting out and feeling cold air on my wet body. There was no better feeling than hot water sprayed hard against my skin. Nothing in the Dingdom comes close to that sensation.

***

There are now somewhere between three million and four million Dings. That's not a lot, when you think about it. Roughly thirty thousand new Dings are collected and activated each year, six hundred per week among all the facilities around the world.

Few people can afford the process, and there are fewer still who want to do it. The main reason people opt out is their religious concern. Like Dar, they prefer the idea of Heaven and hope they will go. Or they believe collection is unnatural and is "playing God," that death is part of God's plan. Many people fear the collection process, wrongfully assuming it might hurt or damage their brain, and others fear the prospect of existing without a body. One man famously said, "If there's no sex, I ain't going."

I have a large group of other Dings with whom I "hang out." Entire societies have formed among Dings around the world. Abliving communities coalesce around almost any tribal dynamic. There is the Lebanese Maronite Writers Group, and Moroccan Atheists for Peace. I am in several societies, including Tech Innovators, Suicide Survivors, ICE (Intermediate Chess Enthusiasts), and Dings Relictus (Dings whose spouses chose not to be collected).

Groups that Livings form change membership often. Few Livings stick with a club or a volunteer job or a board they sit on for more than a few years. Any long-existing group, including such popular singing groups as Nasty Bump, eventually has none of its original members.

A cool aspect of Dingdom is that you can come clean about things you might have kept hidden when you were a Living: sexual orientation, religious belief, economic philosophy, etc. Being an atheist might still not be popular, but you don't have to fear for your life.

I am kind of a big deal in the Dingdom. I never had to worry about being accepted into any group I wanted to join. I have already left several abliving societies. I was never asked to leave because a society gained instant credibility and fame if I were a member.

One of my favorite things about being a Ding is that I can "read" a document or book much faster than I ever could as a Living. Dings' thought processes are cyberfast, operating on a quantum level. Learning new skills or new facts takes almost no time. It means that Dings are better educated than any Living ever could be.

We are not robots, so we are not subject to any of Isaac Asimov's famous Three Laws of Robotics:

First Law—A robot may not injure a human being or, through inaction, allow a human being to come to harm.

Second Law—A robot must obey the orders given it by human beings except where such orders would conflict with the First Law.

Third Law—A robot must protect its own existence as long as such protection does not conflict with the First or Second Law.

I'd have to say that Dings are more dangerous than robots because robots are programmed beings. They were never alive. They can mimic Livings, but their sentience is an act. If it can be programmed in, it can be programmed out. But malevolence in a Ding … that's a different matter, both technically and ethically. I heard about a Ding named Indra Moore who learned how to terminate other Dings. Robots can suffer consequences of their actions, but Dings are harder to punish or to stop if they misbehave.

Dings have several advantages over Livings. We never forget things. We can program ourselves to meet with someone at a specific time, and we will keep that date punctually. I can recall conversations from a hundred years ago as easily as one from last week. It's amazing how much that helps me in dealing with other Dings and with the societies.

We also have perfect "hearing." There's no way to misunderstand words. Once I thought Dar said, "I used a garage." She laughed, "What? No. I said, 'My shoes have arrived'."

The Dingdom offers the possibility of a classless, egalitarian society. There is no illness, no need to raise crops, to hunt, or to gather. There is no difference in appearance or size between me and any other Ding. There are no races. No one is richer or poorer than anyone else. No one is older or younger. The only difference is in intellect, but even there, the access every Ding has to all the accumulated knowledge of humanity gives every Ding equal opportunity. I choose to avail myself of all such opportunities, while I know other Dings who have no curiosity.

There are no dangerous neighborhoods in the Dingdom. There are no cities or, for that matter, no countries. No Ding can harm another, at least not physically. There are no children and no elderly people in need of care.

Why, then, did things go so wrong?

Chapter 37

Nobody—I laugh at that word, since none of us Dings has a body—knows how to be a Ding when they are first activated. Nothing in life prepared us for this strange existence. When I first arrived, I knew more about what to expect than other new Dings, and it still wasn't easy.

I used to love to play music loud, and now, as a Ding, there's no such thing. We can still process sound waves, such as understanding speech, but it's not the same as hearing. It … bothers me, I suppose. Being angry or upset was easier when I was Living; I could "blow off steam" in a lot of ways that were always physical. I would throw something or hit something or yell at someone, or maybe I'd stomp about and go for a brisk walk. A lot of Dings don't cope well with emotions. Good feelings, like love and joy, would often provoke a physical response in Livings. Dings don't have that privilege.

What we do have is down time. It's impossible to be engaged non-stop, and we never sleep, so there are a lot of minutes to fill. New Dings must learn to disengage often. I made sure that this practice was added to the orientation for new arrivals. Dings, like Livings, run out of things to talk about. No matter how much I enjoy a Ding friend, I don't want our visits to last too long (as measured in data exchanged). I break it off after an hour's worth, and even that can be too long. Some Dings I know can't go longer than the equivalent of ten sentences in a conversation.

I figured out a way that we Dings can meditate. We go into a kind of trance. We can be contacted at any time, and we will instantly be attentive, but otherwise we are dormant. I call it "schro." It's a pun on the name Schrödinger—Schro-DING-er—because when you are schro, you're both alert and not alert at the same time. I've been schro for as long as four days in a row. It's a great tool for coping with any overload of emotions. I love that the Dingdom is so quiet; there are no sirens, no horns, and no motors. I wish my life had been so serene.

***

I programmed my Ding so that every time I enter a new conversation or meeting, a few bars of the song "Peaceful Queasy Feeling" by Strangulation plays. I loved that song back Home. (Most Dings now called the world of Livings "Home.") I decided every Ding should be able to pick a theme song that plays, like a fanfare that announces them. I thought it would be a hoot, but it never really caught on.

***

My father told me that video streaming began when he was a young man, and he was overwhelmed at first by the enormously increased selection. I felt overwhelmed in kindergarten when I went to the school library. Where would I begin exploring? I didn't know what I should look for. I usually grabbed the first book I saw next to me, and whatever it was, I was stuck reading it. No one told me I could put it back and make a different choice.

Now imagine how overwhelming the Internet feels when you can access, with few exceptions, every document and recording made for the past two hundred years, and tons of data going back much further than that. When everything is available, nothing is available. It becomes impossible to choose what to do. I've got to back off and go schro to recharge.

***

I underestimated the popularity of watching Living sporting events among Dings. I was not much of a sports fan back Home, so I hadn't thought about how sports could fill the infinite amount of time we Dings have. We have chess and/or bridge tournaments, where Dings compete against each other, but audiences are small for our virtual sports.

Dings' most popular Living sport does not involve any actual humans. It is called Robotball. After American tackle football was banned due to CTE, an entrepreneur named Ajeet Singh designed and built the first androids programmed with the skills of an NFL player. Singh and a group of other billionaires launched the IRFL—the International Robotic Football League. Livings loved it. It was as violent as football and required the same talent and strategy, but no human was harmed. IRFL players were given competitive, playful personalities, but if one of them was mangled on the field, another one could be brought out with the same personality.

Robotball investors made a fortune. People would pay to attend games and companies would sponsor teams around the world, but the economic model was nothing like the NFL. Players did not have to be developed over the course of several years. There was no draft of the best college athletes, and no mind-boggling huge contracts required to recruit top talent. Each robot cost a fraction of the salary that NFL stars had enjoyed.

It was so successful that a competing league was formed in which the players were made more human-like. That proved to be a mistake. Fans became attached to a few of the more colorful robotballers, and when they inevitably were destroyed, viewership plummeted.

I was a huge fan of the Boston Bolts IRFL team. The day they won the Supreme Bowl was one of my happiest days in the Dingdom.

Chapter 38

Klaus Gruber is my new best friend. We met in the Dings Relictus Society. Klaus was collected last year. His wife of nearly fifty years died a few months before he fell ill. She had died unexpectedly and had not been collected in time. Still, he decided to give it a try, not understanding that once you become a Ding, you will probably be around forever. It's not a coat you can try on and return if you don't like it.

Klaus and I have a lot in common. In his native Austria, he developed quantum software for his own small company. He had done well, living in a charming chalet in Salzburg. Like me, he married in his thirties. He and his wife raised two children. They were a family of avid skiers. Their vacations usually involved going to the finest ski resorts around the world. His favorites were Grenoble, Garmisch-Partenkirchen, Tres Valles, Nagano, and Vail. He described each place in detail to me, and then shared videos he made of some downhill adventures. I could almost feel the swoosh of the air around me.

Vivilocution was one of the most revered talents in the Dingdom. It was the ability to describe vividly a thought or fact in such a way that other Dings could experience an emotional reaction. Klaus' accounts of his ski trips made him a master vivilocutor. He had many followers who vicariously enjoyed his exploits.

Klaus and I lived in different eras and cultures, and he had lived about forty years longer than I, but those distinctions are meaningless in the Dingdom. We can talk and brainstorm for long stretches. There is always a new technology we can explore together, or a book or video we could critique.

I discovered that Klaus knows a lot about me. Apparently, he read about perpetuonics and me while he was alive. He knew the history of T.P., and he knew about Laz. I, on the other hand, know nothing about Klaus' history. Perhaps he'll talk with me about it soon.

***

There is no government in the Dingdom. The rules are made and enforced by Livings. I've heard some Dings talk about self-governance, but how would that work? How can we elect or appoint leaders? What would those leaders do? Each society has leaders, following the methods that we all knew as Livings. There's usually a president who organizes and runs the meetings. (We decided long ago to stop saying "chair" a meeting, because Dings have no need for chairs. Instead, we say the leader "stages" the meetings.) There might be a vice president, but we don't need a treasurer. Some societies use a secretary to record a summary of a meeting for Dings who didn't attend.

Among Livings, government leaders make sure the people are fed safe food, provided safe water, protected from the elements and from other people who want to take their land or property or lives. But Dings are already secure, and all their minimal needs are met without the need for governance. I see no reason that should change.

***

I would venture to say that I know my way around the Dingdom better than anyone here. I could navigate the highways and back roads of the Dingdom the way I used to drive around Boston. I have used that to my advantage to meet Dings who were prominent Livings.

I appointed myself as an ambassador of the Dingdom. I make it a point to greet many of the newly activated Dings. Almost everyone here was a Big Deal among Livings. One doesn't accumulate great wealth without having some extraordinary background, even if that wealth was inherited.

Soon after her activation, I had the pleasure of greeting former British Prime Minister Doris Fletcher. She endured tumultuous years in office, what with the deep recession that she inherited, and the water wars in the Middle East and Africa. Climate change literally reshaped Europe and North Africa, creating climate refugees and sowing economic chaos throughout the world. Ms. Fletcher had done a remarkable job of keeping the ship of state afloat.

When she arrived in the Dingdom, she was confused, similar to the common reaction I had experienced. She had endured mild dementia before her collection. Many times, the committee would reject the application of dementia patients to become Dings, but given her stature, they decided to allow it. Her memory lapses included her request to be BRPed, so she had more trouble than most adapting to her new existence. At times, she thought she was still the prime minister, and she demanded to meet with the king of England. Fortunately, no one other than me, and maybe her compadores, heard her make that request.

Back Home, I would have taken someone like Ms. Fletcher on a VIP tour. I'd have shown her the sights around Boston, and maybe taken her to a Red Sox game, baseball rules having been revised to make a game shorter and more entertaining. Here in the Dingdom, there is no "tour" to be given. All that's needed is a brief explanation of how to find things, and most Dings are happy to make their own way.

I had great sympathy for Doris Fletcher. Her life, despite her successes, had been stressful, notably when her husband and son died in a plane crash while she was at a G-14 Summit meeting in Valparaiso. Her combination of strength and vulnerability had touched the world. Now to see this great woman humbled by dementia was heartbreaking. I hoped that T.P. was working on ways to repair the confused bits of Dings like her. I was no longer privy to company priorities.

***

We Dings cherish our memories as much as any Living ever did. We are entirely made of our memories; without them, we don't exist.

One of my favorite memories was meeting Laura Constant, the wealthy grande dame in Antibes, who was our first French Ding. Once I became a Ding, I liked to visit her often, since language was no longer a barrier to our conversations. With translation apps, we could understand each other in real time; no need for an interpreter.

I don't fully understand why I sought Mme. Constant over the dozens of other Livings I had helped to collect. The joy she expressed at the time of her collection had stayed with me.

Laura was delightful. We connected in ways that would have been impossible when we were both living. Without the prospect of our becoming intimate, we could each abandon the games, both flirty and defensive, we might have played had we met *en chair et en os*. She talked with me as an equal. Our former age difference mattered not at all. If I did not know that she died at age eighty-something, I would have sworn I was talking with a strong woman in her prime. For a short time, I wondered if I might have a crush on Laura, but our cultural references were too disparate.

We were laughing over some remark she made, when I said, "That reminds me of a joke I heard. What did the grape say when the elephant stepped on it? Nothing, but it let out a little whine."

Laura was confused. "Why would an elephant step on a grape? Grapes do not grow in countries with elephants, *je pense.*"

I explained why the joke is funny, but she scoffed, "That is not funny at all. My husband was much funnier. He could always make me laugh."

I thought of Dar, and how we used to laugh together all the time, and I knew Laura and I would never share that rapport.

***

I was never a pet lover when I was Living. My mother hated dogs and I was allergic to cats. I never thought about how pet lovers would cope in the Dingdom.

Not well, it turned out. The Petless Society was one of the most active groups in the world of Dings. It got so big, they had to break into chapters to allow everyone a chance to engage. There was the Rottweilers Society and the Lapdogs Society and the Petrified Dings Society and the Reptile Lovers Society. You name it, there was probably a group for it. Pets had been an integral part of people's lives to an extent I underestimated. There was nothing in the Dingdom that could provide them that same level of caring and affection.

I can't tell you how many Dings approached me with questions about collecting their pets. I had to explain why the collection process would not work on other animals (though I suspected it might work on dolphins and certain apes if there were any way to collect them). Some Dings became angry, having expected it would be possible to have Fido or Fluffy by their side again. I was glad that they could not physically attack me for ruining their fantasies.

Chapter 39

Once I had gotten my bearings and accustomed myself to my new and forever existence, I sought some of the people I had helped enter the Dingdom. One of my first visits was with U.S. Senator Mark Rasmussen.

"What do you think?" I asked. "How are you enjoying your life as a Ding?"

"It's everything I could have hoped for," he said. "You know, as a Living, I was always confronting problems, albeit trivial ones. Take my house, for example, which was a half-century old when I bought it. I could never relax and enjoy it; something always needed attention ... and money. Replace the roof, paint the walls, repair the plumbing, upgrade the stove. It wore me out. And now, well, nothing ever goes wrong in the Dingdom."

"I'm glad you feel that way, and I'm anxious to discover it for myself, from the inside now," I mused.

He said, "There's another aspect I didn't appreciate at first. Most of the world hated us Americans. We treated them horribly, and yet, they wanted to have the good life we enjoyed, the life they saw us living in videos."

I chuckled. "What they saw in videos did not jibe with the Americans they encountered in real life, the soldiers and the tourists and the businessmen come to make more money than they could ever use."

"I traveled a great deal back Home," Rasmussen said, "and

I felt their hatred of what I stood for. It took some getting used to the Dingdom, where there is no poverty, no clash of cultures. The equality we thought we had there truly exists here. I love this place."

***

I got to greet Garland (they/them) Holiday (not their name at birth). Garland back Home was a "bisexual activist." They led an influential group whose goal was to destigmatize the LGBTQIA community. After a hundred years, they still had work to do. Garland had led the organization for more than forty years when they died. They had fascinating stories to tell me.

Garland was not concerned only with freedom regardless of sexual identity or orientation. They also advocated for people to engage in more sexual activity outside of a monogamous marriage. "Marriage is an obsolete vestige of the Patriarchy," they told me almost as soon as we met.

The realities of the Dingdom were a shock to Garland's core. "No way to have sex here?" they moaned. When I told them that gender no longer mattered here, they thought I was joking. That became another source of their depression.

Depression among Dings was the first sign that perpetuonics is not a perfect science, nor can it lead to the full Utopia I envisioned. I still felt that most of Utopia was likely to endure.

Some depressed Dings became bitter and complained frequently to anyone who would listen. Some others asked for termination. Some became introspective and a few became prodigiously creative. I was surprised that more Dings, freed from the rigors of living, were unable or unwilling to try their virtual hand at creativity.

Garland withdrew from the Dingdom for over a year. They never came to meetings of other Dings. They never talked with occasional visitors in the nearest Lounge. They would not reply to any communications. Yet I could tell that Garland was still activated when I checked the compadores' log.

After their year of isolation, Garland Holiday emerged. I heard from them directly. They wanted my help in understanding the communication networks of the Dingdom. They began to engage with thousands of societies, advocating for a return to sexual thinking. Most societies dismissed and even banned Garland. I heard much grumbling from Dings who said that we were better off without sexual lives, given how much it screwed up Home.

I stopped checking on Garland after a while, and they never contacted me. I wonder how their campaign for virtual sex is going. No one else is talking about it.

***

When I was Living, I played solitaire games on my tablet whenever I had a free minute. As a Ding, I play even more. It would have been easy to join group games, such as bridge and role-playing games, but I value my alone time too much to give it to strangers.

Some games keep track of your progress. I rarely pay attention to those statistics, but I was amazed when I noticed that I had played more than a hundred thousand rounds of Canfield. Without the brightness of day or the darkness of night, it's easy to lose a sense of time.

It's also easy to lose a sense of self. There are no mirrors in the Dingdom. As a Living, I took mirrors for granted. They were everywhere, and I, like most people, grew used to seeing myself reflected in them. Not a day went by when I did not see my reflection; I knew how I looked and memorized every feature of my face. As a Ding, I had no physical appearance. I did not look like anything, though others could see my avatar based on a photo of me that was now more than a hundred years old.

I remember my father telling me not to marry a woman based on her beauty. "Beauty fades," he said. "A shiny new car looks great, but the car you'll love the most is the rusty old one you've had for years." I loved the way Dar looked, but I married her based on how well we got along. We saw the world the same way, at least until Laz got sick.

Now, in the Dingdom, beauty was manifest only in one's personality. There was no such thing as physical beauty. You liked someone for their thoughts, or not at all. For Dings who had lived a long life, that was customary. For younger Dings like me, it was revolutionary.

Speaking of beauty, I decided to visit Carlotta Silverstone, whom I had not thought of in years. She was the first totally blind Living to become a Ding and to discover she had vision in the Dingdom. I had been alive when she was collected at age eighty-two. She had been surprised to see that she was beautiful in her twenties and thirties.

Carlotta told me that the Dingdom had been a miracle for her and for countless people who had a disability when Living. People who had been deaf could communicate as easily in the Dingdom as anyone else. People with mobility issues no longer had trouble "getting around."

"The surprising thing is," she told me, "I still think of myself as a blind person, although I've spent more years here than I did back Home. It became part of my identity. I almost miss it, my blindness. Isn't that curious?"

Chapter 40

I have big news. A man named Jafir Mbonoku has figured out a way to add memories of physical sensations when collecting a Living. He worked with a prosthetic skin manufacturer to develop neodermis for Dings. When a Living touches the neodermis that is wired to the systems in the Lounge, a Ding can "feel" the touch. The brand name for the neodermis is Pelletan™, roughly meaning "skin touch."

I have two problems with this amazing invention. First, it is not retroactive; the memories of touch must be collected with the rest of the data. So, I won't be able to experience touch again.

Second, the stimulus on the neodermis can come only from a Living. There is no way for another Ding to "stroke" the neodermis virtually. In other words, simulated sex between Dings will not be possible.

The introduction of neodermis to Lounges, which is still awaiting approval from T.P.'s policy board and perpetuonics regulators, is not without controversy. Some compadores have already objected to it, expecting that their abliving charges will expect them to stroke the Pelletan in a sexual manner.

An unholy collaboration of psychotherapists and fundamentalist clerics warn that giving abliving beings the ability to experience physical pleasure and pain will open a Pandora's box that many Dings hoped to escape.

I have mixed feelings about pursuing Mbonoku's invention.

When I first learned of it, I was immediately jealous of those future Dings who might not have to sacrifice physical sensations. I wished it might happen to me. On the other hand, as a creator of and philosopher about the Dingdom, I could see the myriad problems it would introduce to our nearly perfect existence. As the old saying goes, "If it ain't broke, don't fix it."

Chapter 41

I came closer to falling in love with Maria Grushinova than with any other Ding. I guess I did fall in love with her.

I have now been many more years without Dar than we were together back Home. At some point, I realized that my future would never include Dar, and that I should move on. What was holding me back? Shouldn't Dar be a "distant memory" now? But she's not. My memories of her are as strong as ever.

One thing about becoming a Ding I failed to anticipate was how my memory would affect me differently. For a Living, vivid memories fade. "It's a distant memory," people say, metaphorically referencing the effect of seeing something from far away. I thought that was how memory worked: long-ago experiences are all but forgotten, or are remembered as if seen through gauze. That's not how it goes in the Dingdom. A memory, once collected, is entirely fresh unless it has been deliberately erased. Dings cannot develop dementia. Events that seem ancient to Livings are perfectly current to me. I understand that they happened long ago, but all the details are as fresh and crisp as an apple eaten right off the tree.

Moving on from Dar was, therefore, harder than I'd expected. I could relive virtually all our time together until the day I was collected. If she had allowed herself to be collected, I'd have waited for her. That might have been a mistake, though. I met other Dings whose spouses were collected a few years later, and when they were reunited, the earlier Ding found that their loved one had remarried and felt closer to spouse #2. It was heartbreaking.

I was thrilled to meet Maria. She was yet-another rich person when she arrived. I had never heard of her; we met through a society. I was astounded by the ideas she shared at meetings. No one else I'd met had the unique perspectives she regularly expressed.

For example, Maria recounted an experience she'd had recently. She saw her compadore flip a light switch, and she remembered how, as a Living, she would walk into a room and unconsciously reach for a light switch. "One time, I was surprised when I inadvertently turned the light off, not realizing it was already on. It's a perfect example of the unconscious mind of a Living. My conscious mind was thinking about something else, but my unconscious prompted that automatic reflex of reaching for the switch. When I recalled that time, I realized I no longer have an unconscious mind. Dings are nothing but conscious activity."

We talked about dreaming. I had often loved my dreams; I would tell Dar about the most vivid ones. There was something exciting and surreal in waking up from a dream and taking a moment to separate my wakeful mind from my dreaming mind, to come back to life. "Where did those visions come from?" I had wondered aloud. How was I able to concoct and visualize fantastic, surreal places and events? Dreaming happened so easily; there was nothing I had to do to make myself dream about a rock band and a flying train and a talking tooth.

Maria was right; we Dings have no unconscious mind. We do not dream. I lost that gift without realizing it. What was it Shakespeare said? "To sleep, perchance to dream." Yes, it was from Hamlet: "In this sleep of death, what dreams may come?" Now I knew the answer: none.

The last time I had been so excited by a woman's strong, wise personality was when Dar and I were Livings; we both had bodies. I could see Dar. She had a faint aroma that made me want to stand closer to her. "Pheromones," I surmised. Her face appealed to me, probably reminding me of a favorite aunt back in Weymouth. I wanted to hold her as soon as we met. It was animal behavior, beyond my control, though, of course, I controlled it.

Now, there was no body. Maria—who asked me to call her Masha—had no shape, no smell, no soft skin, no physical qualities at all except the virtual face and voice the computer generated. So, what would I fall in love with? I thought of Livings who are both deaf and blind. They fall in love. They have families and make children. What is the source of their attraction to another Living?

Can you love a personality with no person attached? Can you fall in love with a set of ideas and principles in the abstract, disembodied? I loved words and stories I had read, fictional characters with no more tangible qualities than Masha. I realized, to my surprise, that the same thoughts expressed so forcefully by a man could be as intoxicating. If I could fall in love with bodyless Masha, couldn't I also fall in love with Misha or Mick or Stanley?

Another old memory came flooding back. I was fourteen, hanging around outside the high school after dark as a concert by a students' rock band ended (part of a talent night the PTO organized each fall). Several kids I knew were with me. Most of them were vaping THC. There was a seventeen-year-old named Chip whom I watched maneuvering his way close to me. I didn't understand why, because we didn't really know each other. He was a senior, the only one talking with me and my friends. We were mostly freshmen with a few sophs. I was talking to a girl named Bella, whom I liked. When two other girls said they had to get home, Bella went with them, and within a minute everyone but me and Chip was gone. I leaned against the school wall. Chip came over and leaned against it about a dozen centimeters from me.

We were in the shadows. The lights that bathed the driveway at the front of the school couldn't find me as I prepared to walk home.

He leaned forward and swung his body around to face me.

"Hi, I'm Chip," he said.

"I know," I answered.

"Who are you? You're a freshman, right?"

"Right. I'm Declan."

"Is that your girlfriend? You know, that croissant you were talking to?" ("Croissant" was the latest slang term for a cute girl, because it's a great shape and it's edible. Hey, don't blame me; I didn't make that up!)

"No. Well, I mean we're friends, but …"

"But she's nothing special, huh?"

I didn't say anything, but I was getting an uneasy feeling about Chip.

Chip said, "Hey, that last band was really good, huh? The drummer, Theo, he's one of my best friends."

"Huh," I grunted.

"You might want to meet him. He's a cool guy. You should see his forearms. God, they're so thick with muscles. He, uh … we work out together."

"Oh." I could not think of anything else to say. I kind of hoped he'd get the hint, that I was not worth talking to, but he wouldn't quit.

"You could work out with us if you wanted," Chip added. I didn't know if it was pathetic or flattering.

"I, uh … should go. Parents, you know."

"I'll walk with you, Dec. Can I call you 'Dec'?"

"I can go myself." I didn't want to let him give me a pet name.

"Naw, c'mon. I'll just walk with you down to the main road."

"Whatever."

We walked in silence. Maybe he got the message that I'm not exciting, and I'm not interested in whatever he wants.

"You want to go see Theo and the band again next Friday after the football game?"

"Um …"

Chip stepped in front of me, and I stopped. No one was

around. No one could see us.

"What?" I asked.

"I want to see you again." He shuffled towards me. He was about six inches taller than I, and he was athletically built. He reached up and touched the collar of my jacket, and I flinched.

"Don't," I said. "Please don't."

"I'm not gonna hurt you, you know."

"I know, but you want to …"

"I want to kiss you, you mean? Yeah, but not tonight. Tonight, you can go home to Mommy and Daddy." He was getting snippy as he sensed rejection.

"I'm sorry," I said, though I felt he should be the one apologizing.

"It's okay. Maybe another time. Think about it, huh?" Chip walked straight ahead past me, back towards the school. I suppose he had a car there.

Think about it? That's all I did for the next month. Does he know something about me that I don't know? Do I send out gay vibes? Am I cute to gay guys, 'cause I don't think the girls find me cute? Am I gay because I thought about Chip all the time that month? Not in a sexual way, but as someone who came on to me, which was the first time ever. How do you not think about that when you're fourteen years old?

I never ran into Chip again, but I saw him with some guys outside school a couple of times. He looked at me once for a second, and then looked away.

When my society meeting ended and Masha went on her way that first time, I thought about Chip walking away. It was a strange time to remember him. I wondered if he were somewhere in the Dingdom.

Chapter 42

Kim Wong-Yoo had invented the Tempellium™, the first car battery that could be fully recharged in about ten seconds. It had revolutionized transportation. Special "tempels" had sprung up across the country and around the world. A car running on "empty" could recharge faster than ancient petrol-guzzling vehicles could refill a tank. A tempel is even faster than a hydrogen-refilling station, and best of all, it does not draw its energy from the electric grid.

Mr. Kim had become one of the richest people on Earth thanks to his ingenuity. His investors were similarly rewarded. When he arrived in the Dingdom, he expected to be treated like a superstar. He wasn't. There is equity in the Dingdom that does not exist back Home. The deference a new Ding receives is entirely up to their compadore, and most compadores learned that it's a mistake to treat any Ding as special.

Although I had created the Dingdom, I had no special status here. I knew the technology better than most, but no one in charge came to me for advice … or permission. The only nod to my celebrity was a class I taught about perpetuonics. I led the class on an irregular basis, so attendance was small.

Kim was a troublemaker from the moment he was activated. He tried to boss everyone around, and I heard he made two compadores cry. I sent him an anonymous message that said I know how to terminate a Ding permanently, and that I would terminate him if he continued to bully everyone around him, both Living and Ding. I guess he got the message, because he settled down and was a lot more cooperative. I had never bullied someone before. It had worked, and I felt glad about that. Then I felt guilty about being glad.

***

I began to see Masha every day. I had not been this happy or energized (if you can say that about a being that does not consume energy) in decades. I imagined that if I were a Living, my bones would ache to be near her.

When I was first activated, I would ask to see images, particularly videos, of new Dings when I met them, and I would show them how I had looked and sounded as a Living. I soon realized that the Dingdom considered it poor form and it was a bad idea. No one's Living images looked as I expected, and it was impossible to know if someone shared their actual self. Years later, T.P. figured out how to animate a lifelike avatar based on the Ding's appearance. Deep-fake likenesses had been around even before I was born, but T.P.'s innovation was to make a face and torso that was fully controlled by abliving thoughts.

Back Home, it had been easy for people you met online to disguise their true appearance, but any deception fell apart the moment you met in real life. I had met people who were older or heavier or even a different race than the images they'd initially shared. Yet in the Dingdom, unless you dug through digital archives, you could not know for sure how a Ding used to look.

I'd been courting Masha for months before my curiosity overwhelmed me. I said, "I love all our time together. I know you were fifty-six when you were collected. You've told me a lot about your life and your family. Is it wrong of me to want to see pictures of you and them?"

Masha laughed. "I've wondered the same about you, but I

was afraid to ask."

"My avatar isn't really how I picture myself; I don't want you to see my old corporate ID photo. It was probably in the T.P. literature when you signed up to be collected."

"I don't think it was," she said.

One of my compadores interrupted. "Declan, you shouldn't be asking Maria for her images, but I can't stop her from showing them if she wants to."

"Right," I answered. "You can't."

"But you should know that T.P. no longer uses your picture on their brochures or website unless you dig deep into its history."

I had long ago abandoned most of my ego, but that news stung. Perpetuonics was my legacy. I was proud of it, but newer Dings knew little or nothing about me. The Livings who knew me were long dead. A few had been collected, but I never heard from them. For the first time, I felt I was truly dead and gone from Home. The Dingdom was now my domain, and if I wanted to be important here, I could not rely on my past achievements.

Masha said, "I always hated my body. I knew it was foolish of me, but I absolutely hated it. It had hair where I didn't want hair. It had a round belly when all I wanted was a flat one. It had a beak instead of a nose. I was too tall for some boys and too short for others."

"And now you are just right," I said, hoping the flattery would elicit a favorable response.

"I am not going to show you how I looked when I was young, but you can see this picture of me taken at my fifty-fifth birthday, when I no longer cared how horrible I looked."

She shared a file with a picture of her standing by the door of a house. She was shorter than I'd imagined, but she had a nice smile. Her nose did not appear overly large. "Nice!" I said. "You look happy."

"I was happy. I was ... happy. There's no other word for it."

"You outlived me by a lot," I told her. "I don't know what I'd have looked like if I'd lived to be ninety."

"Oh, go ahead and show me a picture. I can tell you're dying to."

I showed her a picture of Dar and Laz and me, my favorite one that a friend took when we were all at a picnic.

"That's lovely," Masha said. "Who's the little girl?"

"He's a boy. That's Laz, our son."

"You never told me you have a son. Is he in the Dingdom, too?"

"No. He died. Really young. Almost three years old."

"Oh no! That's terrible. Oh, Declan...."

"He got sick. Covid-36. Before your time."

"My time," she mused. "Wow. He'd have been older than I am. He looks so little."

I felt the trauma of Laz's death for the first time in a hundred years. "He was perfect. I ... I couldn't take it when he died. I guess I killed myself."

There was silence.

"Masha?"

"Yes, I heard you. I didn't ... I under ... No, I don't understand, but I get it. I felt that way when my husband died."

"Tell me about him."

"Yevgeny. That was his name. He was everything to me, the only man I ever loved. The only man worth loving. He died in an explosion. He was never collected."

"What kind of explosion?" I asked.

"I don't want to talk about it," Masha stated, making it clear she meant it.

"Did you have children?"

"Yes, a boy and a girl. They are still Living. They're very old now."

"Maybe I can meet them someday."

"I am lonely here. I was not so social back Home in Moscow. I did my job, I went home, I had a few friends. I read a lot of books. A lot of books. And now I'm here."

"With me. You're here with me."

"Yes. With you."

Chapter 43

My dad died when I was a senior in high school. The principal came into the Student Council's biweekly meeting and signaled me to leave the room with him. As I walked to the door, I pondered what I could possibly have done wrong. He told me that my father had died at work, he didn't know any details, and that I should go home immediately. One of the math teachers was prepared to drive me if I didn't want to drive myself, but I declined the offer. On Graduation Day, when I got my diploma, I held up a sign that said, "This is for my Dad."

***

The speaker said, "Do you know what real freedom is? It is keeping dominion over yourself. You cannot give anyone dominion over you. Why did you obey the laws when you were alive? Not because you necessarily agreed with those laws, but because you didn't want to be punished. When someone else has the right to punish you, they control you. They have dominion over you. And being a Ding is like that. Being a Ding means you can never have freedom. I have been given eternal life in exchange for my freedom. I'd say that was a poor bargain."

Devontreus Jackson, a member of the Dings Relictus society where I met Klaus and Masha, was our speaker. He was an activist among Dings, building a controversial reputation.

I was floored by his statement. We Dings have so much freedom. We're free from our bodies and our need to eat, to make a living, to fix things. I interrupted. "You're wrong. The Dingdom gives us eternal life and freedom."

"Declan," he said, "you're not the best judge of the Dingdom."

"But I created it."

"Cheers, Mate," he said, mocking me. "It's not yours anymore. It evolved. Whatever you thought you created, it's not that now."

"What do you mean you can never have freedom? What does that mean?" I hoped he would explain it. "Does anybody else know what you mean? Because I sure don't."

Devontreus seemed to snort. I took it as a gesture of impatience with me, but he couldn't dodge the question with the society listening in. "It's a question of control. To be completely free, there cannot be anyone who controls you. T.P. is totally in control here. We Dings have no ability to govern ourselves, but we have that right and should be given a say. Remember 'Taxation without representation is tyranny?' We've got our bloody compadores butting in anytime they feel like it, which is anytime they're alerted that you're violating their rules."

"But the rules are there to protect us! I wrote a lot of those rules."

"Like I said, we make sacrifices. We give up some of our freedom to have them protect us. Maybe you're okay with that deal, but I'm not. We should be treated like individuals with all the rights we had as Livings and more. I could give on a couple of things, like not bullying other Dings, but they don't stop there. They want more and more control, and if we don't like it, they can terminate us."

"No, they can't! I never allowed that. I had lots of safeguards so that wouldn't happen."

He scoffed. "'Wouldn't happen' you thought. But as long as it could happen, as long as it is not physically impossible, it will happen … and it has happened."

I knew he was right about it being technically possible. Everyone knew he was right, which made denying it out of the question. But he continued, "Even if they don't terminate you outright, they can selectively edit your collection data, remove some behaviors they don't like."

"Absolutely not!" I cried. "Unless you ask them to erase a memory that's causing you pain, it's totally forbidden."

"Maybe it was when you were in charge, but that's ancient history. Whoever's running things now is slicing and dicing Dings."

"How do you know that?"

"Ask Maria."

***

Masha and I disconnected from the society meeting so we could talk privately.

"What did Devontreus mean?" I asked as gently as I could, hoping there was a simple explanation.

"I don't know."

"I think you do."

"You're right. I'm a terrible liar."

"What happened?"

"Remember I told you my husband died in an explosion?"

"Yes, and you didn't want to talk about it."

She paused. "Because it's not true. I made it up."

"How did he die? And why would you make up something like that?" I asked.

"I don't want him to find me."

"So, he's a Ding?"

"Yes. He died after me. He has been looking for me."

"How did you find out?"

"My compadore told me. She wasn't supposed to, but she slipped up."

"What did she tell you?"

"That Yevgeny should not have qualified to be collected. He should not be here."

"Why?"

"Because he killed me. I didn't know it, of course, until she told me. I was obviously collected before I was murdered. I have no awareness of my death."

I had never encountered a murder victim in the Dingdom, but there must be others, and none of them would have a memory of their demise. The situation creates an ethical dilemma: Should Dings be told how and by whom they lost their life? If they died peacefully, we never hesitated to let them know. I knew about my suicide, so why wasn't Masha told about her husband as soon as she was activated?

I said, "Your compadore didn't tell you right away?"

"No. I found out yesterday, and I told Devontreus. That's one of the things he was upset about when he talked about our lack of freedom."

"Yevgeny hasn't tried to contact you yet?"

"I don't think so. I got pinged by someone a couple of days ago, but they canceled before I could see any data on them."

"Your compadores can request Protection from Abuse, hiding you from him behind an invisible firewall. He won't see you behind the wall; he won't even see the wall."

"She told me she did that, but I am still worried. What if he finds me? What can he do to me here? He murdered me once, so …"

I thought of the stories of Indra Moore terminating her fellow Dings. Masha faced unprecedented jeopardy. She could be killed twice by the same person, something I feel confident saying never occurred back Home. I had to make sure he could not harm her.

Protecting murdered Dings would become my mission, I decided, but first I had to use my knowledge of the Dingdom to get rid of Yevgeny.

I told Klaus about Masha's problem. Between the two of us, I thought, we'd figure out a way to locate Yevgeny and deactivate him. I didn't like the idea of terminating another Ding, but I could think of no other way to prevent him from finding Masha eventually.

Klaus was the first to raise an important point: What if Masha were misinformed or, worse, lying about her husband? We had only her word that Yevgeny had killed her, and that he was now somewhere in the Dingdom. If that's what the compadore told her, how did the compadore know? After all, nothing was said when Masha was activated. Perhaps nothing was said because there was no truth to the tale.

Chapter 44

I had no influence left at T.P. None of the current administrators had been alive when I was in charge. The Dingdom had changed, but the technological basics were the same as always. I could find my way around and bypass some of the so-called "forebays" that were meant to prevent unauthorized trespass.

First, Klaus and I researched the news media of Livings to find stories about Yevgeny. There was no obituary, so either he was still alive, or no one cared enough to write one. If he had been collected before he died, T.P would not have known about his death and would not have activated him. Then we found obituaries for Maria Grushinova. There was no mention of her being murdered. It said she was survived by her husband, Yevgeny. At least that part was true. Did she deliberately lie to me, or had she been misled by her compadore? It would be illegal for Masha's compadores to talk with me about her, so I must ask Masha directly. It pained me to have to confront her, knowing it might end our relationship.

Livings cannot experience the twenty-four-hour existence of Dings. Dings don't need to sleep, so we can conduct business any time, and visit with our compadores or other Dings. We never get tired, although some Dings apparently get bored, a status I never share. There are no breaks for mealtime or using the bathroom or grabbing a snack. It takes us microseconds to research things. We Dings are constrained only by our imaginations.

I have found that Dings, despite having access to nearly the entire library of human thought, tend to retain the beliefs and opinions they had at collection. Liberals remain liberal, conservatives remain conservative, and everything in between stays as it was. I have encountered ablivings who insist that Nelson Mandela is still alive in a bunker in Namibia.

Truth is fluid in the Dingdom, so I was unsure about trusting Masha. There is no "body language" to give away falsehoods. A simulated voice might not betray a nervous speaker. The traditional lie detector Livings use relies on physiological measurements, which had no relevance in the Dingdom. Attempts had been made over the years to analyze a Ding's psychic patterns to detect lying, but nothing had worked well yet. I had no choice but to hope she would be honest with me. I waited until she had completed a visit with her compadore.

"I need to ask you something," I began.

"Is it about Yevgeny?" she guessed.

"Yes."

"You don't believe me, do you?"

"I … I don't know what to think. The information about your death is confusing."

"I know," she admitted. "I believed it when I told you that he killed me. Then I got to thinking about your reaction, so I researched it myself. I found out that I died in a car accident. Yevgeny had nothing to do with it."

"Then why did you believe he did?" I wondered.

"One of my compadores told me. I had no reason to doubt her. She seemed alarmed and frightened for me."

Aspects of perpetuonics have been refined and improved since I died. One of the most impressive changes is that by using AI, Dings can communicate through an advanced avatar complete with vocal intonations, presumably conveying the talker's mental process. Should one word or phrase be emphasized? Is sarcasm intended? Other Dings can observe that avatar the same way they observe Living visitors to a Lounge, parsing speech and facial expressions. Masha's avatar was visibly upset.

I said, "Okay, Masha, I believe you now. But it raises the question of how and why your compadore lied to you. What's her name?"

"Will she be in trouble?"

"She'll be investigated, that's for sure. Trouble depends on what happened."

"I really like her, Declan. I really ... her name is Viktoria."

"Which Perpetual Care Center is hers?"

"The one in Novomoskovsky Okrug."

I was exasperated. "It's fine that you like her, Masha, but what she has done is so far out of bounds that it may be a crime. She will lose her job."

"Can't you prevent that?" she pleaded.

"No, I can't, and I wouldn't. Did she tell you why she lied to you about something so important?"

"She doesn't know I know. I didn't tell her yet."

"Masha, you must tell me the truth. Did she tell you that Yevgeny murdered you and that he was hunting for you here in the Dingdom?" I so hoped Masha was innocent.

"Yes. She said, 'Do you know how you died? Do you know your husband murdered you?' And I said, 'How would I know that?'"

I replied, "Your arrival orientation should have covered anything as important as that. It's strange to experience your own death as something that happened to another person, isn't it?"

Masha's avatar smiled. "I thought I was the only one who felt that way. I cannot relate at all to the woman I was."

"Especially if you thought she was murdered by Yevgeny. Which is what I'm saying. You were told something different at your orientation. I should have known that they would not accidentally omit a murder. It never happened. Viktoria lied to you, and there must be a reason."

"I am so angry with her," said Masha.

"Don't confront her. Not yet," I cautioned. "I may not have influence, but I know who to contact about this. Remember that Viktoria's a Living, so she can still escape if she gets spooked."

"What is 'spooked'? What does that mean?"

I said, "Afraid, like she saw a ghost."

"I will not spook her then. Why would she do this to me?"

I reached out to the proper department at Transitions Perpetuonics headquarters. Within two days, Viktoria had been arrested.

Viktoria, it turned out, had an affair with Yevgeny a couple of years before Maria died. The affair ended badly. Yevgeny cut it off and warned Viktoria to leave him alone. Then she found herself as one of Masha's compadores, and she planned her revenge. She would go see Yevgeny and beg him to take her back, and if he didn't, she was going to poison him and make sure he would never reconnect with Masha.

Yevgeny was still alive. Police officers told him about Viktoria's plot. He showed up in the Lounge and asked to visit with Masha.

She told him, "I am glad to see you are not dead, Yevgeny."

"Thank you, my darling," he said. "I am so sorry ..."

She cut him off. "No, you are sorry only that you got caught. Nice girlfriend you picked. She is a crazy *suka*."

"I know!" he protested. "Why do you think I dumped her?"

Masha was livid, if that's possible for a Ding. "So, if she wasn't crazy, you'd have kept sleeping with her?"

"You didn't know about it until after you were dead! Why should you be upset now?"

"That was the wrong thing to say, Zhenya."

He doubled down. "What you didn't know about didn't hurt you."

"What else did I not know about? How many other whores did you chase?"

He did not know how to quit when he was behind. He said, "It was your fault, Masha. You were no good at the sex. What was I supposed to do?"

"Oh no," she shouted. "You are not blaming anything on me. It was all your doing."

"I admit I was with her. Let it go," he begged.

"You can't even say you're sorry, you dick. *Poshyol ty*! Get out of here, and don't come back!"

"Why would I come back? You're dead and I'm out here, and now I will sleep with as many women as I want."

"Good for you! And one day, when you're dead, don't come looking for me. What would I want with a dried-up old prune like you?"

He stood up and turned towards the camera as he prepared to storm out of the Lounge. "You'll be begging me to come visit you, but you can rot in hell." He left.

I was anxious to hear about Masha's meeting with Yevgeny. I had to hope she would report it to me accurately. I waited for her to reach out.

Masha contacted me the day after her fight with Yevgeny. She was contrite, yet her spirits had not waned. "I'm here in the Dingdom as I planned. I have my whole life ahead of me." I wanted so much to hug her to my chest.

She was not the first Ding to express similar sentiments. It felt as if we'd been reborn, and with no possibility of dying, the future seemed limitless.

Chapter 45

I have not listened to a weather report in a hundred years. There is no weather in the Dingdom. It feels like every day is a sunny day, although it's pitch black unless we visit a Lounge or search the Internet for images. I'm still astonished how our digital brains can convert data into an image or video, including ones we've never seen.

If I had to pinpoint what caused the Dingdom to unravel, it was when T.P. went away from the principles on which I founded the Dingdom: Respect, Equality, Fairness.

I wanted to know more about Devontreus Jackson, but based on my last conversation with him, I was afraid to ask him directly. So, I did my own sleuthing.

He owned a chain of PTV dealerships in Atlanta. A PTV is a Personal Transportation Vehicle. My original business partner, Twibil, still makes PTV's. Jackson repped several PTV brands, and he made a fortune. As a Living, he was used to being in charge. Perhaps the Dingdom was too egalitarian for his liking.

Devontreus was again holding forth at a Dings Relictus Society meeting.

"I did not allow myself to be collected so I could become enslaved," he said.

I was having none of that. "You chose to be collected; no one did it against your will. Comparing the Dingdom to slavery is offensive, to be honest with you."

"That's because you are part of the patriarchy that collected us with false promises and whitewashing the problems Dings face."

A few other members grunted their approval.

I needed to win them over, and anger wouldn't do it. "Look, I get that the Dingdom is not what you expected. I'm a Ding, too, and I have been surprised by so many things here. And there is a lot of good stuff. We can't expect perfection."

Devontreus scoffed. "Perfection? The Dingdom isn't even close to perfection. I'd settle for half decent, but it's not even that good."

"Okay, tell me what it is you want to do but can't. Maybe together we can lodge a protest and get some changes made."

"You have no power here, Declan. You're as impotent as the rest of us."

"Maybe I—"

He cut me off. "For one thing, I want to be able to speak without my compadores listening in, like they probably are right now."

"That's for your protection," I said.

"How? How does my lack of privacy protect me?"

I hesitated. "Well, it's, uh ..."

He didn't wait for me to think of something. "When you were living, would you have let the police or the FBI listen in to your phone conversations without a warrant, without at least probable cause? No, you wouldn't. And they couldn't search your house, either, unless they had evidence you committed a crime."

"Well ... you're right," I said. "I didn't think of it that way."

"No one does. Everyone is willing to give up some amount of freedom for the illusion of security. But we don't need security in the Dingdom. Everyone is already dead and can't be punished further, except ..."

"Except?" I asked.

"Except for what's happening now, which is involuntary reduction."

"What?"

"That's what I call it when T.P. edits your Ding and removes the parts they don't like."

"They're not allowed to do that," I protested.

"For a smart guy, you're pretty naïve."

I said, "I prefer to think of it as optimistic. I want to think the best of everyone."

He shrugged me off. "You asked me what I want to do that's forbidden. For one thing, we can't even work if we want to. Not meaningful work, anyway."

"That's not true. There are Dings doing lots of things, like programming, graphic design, writing. T.P. has to make sure our labor is not exploited, since we can't get paid. They can't let companies give the jobs of Livings to us Dings."

"That's not the work I had in mind."

"So, like what?"

"I was a salesman. I want to sell stuff."

"What stuff?"

"Anything I want. I can still sell PTV's, or real estate, or—"

I felt my respect for him waning. "No, you can't. You can't sell anything to Livings."

"For my descendants. I can still contribute to the family, even if I can't use the money. I know how to sell things. I'm good at it."

I sighed, or at least I felt like I sighed. "Devontreus, I get it. It's fine you want to help your family, but you can't. It's unethical."

He exploded. "Why? Why is it unethical? Because you said so? Who gets hurt by it?"

"You do. You'd open up all kinds of fraud and exploitation."

"So, what? I can protect myself."

"No, that's not the point. You're the one who could commit fraud. Dings can't sign contracts because there's no appropriate enforcement mechanism. If you cheat someone, what can they do to you?"

"Then I'll just handle the sale and a Living can handle the contracts."

"It's not going to work," I said emphatically.

"I don't have to take your word for it. You don't get to decide these things anymore."

"You're right; I don't. But I know how the system works."

"I've already told my compadore I want to appeal. I'll get a Living lawyer and sue if I have to."

That was the last time I heard from or spoke to Devontreus. Maybe he was right about T.P.'s ability to terminate Dings.

PART FOUR
Devolution

"It was built against the will of the immortal gods, so it did not last for long."

— Homer, *The Iliad*

Chapter 46

Dings noticed when Devontreus Jackson failed to join several Relictus meetings in a row. Questions were asked. Had anyone talked with him? Apparently not.

We are not given access to details about individual Dings, only general demographic data about the Dingdom. I have no idea how many Dings there are in each of the Perpetual Care Centers. The Dingdom is at least as large as some of the more populous cities in the world. I don't know why T.P. wants to keep the numbers secret. Perhaps they are no longer encouraging collection of Livings, but why would that be?

I met Angelika Žemyna through Masha, who was now my constant companion. Angelika, like Masha, had been collected at the Novomoskovsky Okrug Perpetual Care Center. One of the compadores there introduced them.

Angelika was angry when Devontreus disappeared. She was inclined, she said, to act, and she had something in the works. She had been in the Dingdom several years longer than Masha. Angelika knew the ropes as well as any Ding I'd met here. Apparently, she had worked for T.P. in Russia before she died.

***

To my surprise, I was asked to report to my Lounge to meet with an unnamed Living, someone who had requested my attention. My compadore—the thirty-first compadore I'd had over these many years—said he would not be monitoring that meeting. I soon found out why.

Waiting for me was Merrill Winesap, T.P.'s executive vice president in charge of security. He said he was looking for someone in the Dingdom who could monitor "aberrant activity" and report it to him. He knew I had protected the system when I turned in Viktoria, the compadore who had betrayed Masha. I had done nothing disloyal to T.P. in all the years since I'd been collected, and he felt I was the perfect source in the Dingdom to protect T.P.

Would I be the first spy in the Dingdom? After all these years, and after the mishegoss with Devontreus, I assumed there had been others. Another Ding could be spying on me right now. How would I know? Intelligence gathering in the Dingdom is nothing like Home. There are no shadows to hide in, no smuggling of documents or thumb drives. There are no wiretaps or bugs to install. The snooping here would be less obvious. I could access data with few restraints or privacy controls, despite what most Dings had been told.

I told Winesap I would do it, though I already knew I was more inclined to be loyal to my fellow Dings than to T.P. Perhaps as his literal insider, I'd become a double agent, able to keep tabs on Transitions Perpetuonics' motives. I wondered if he knew about my relationship with Masha, and whether she might be on my watchlist.

When we met, Winesap said, "There's an existential threat to the Dingdom that we must eliminate now, before it grows. New societies are forming, and some of them are disturbing."

I said, "Are you concerned about the Dings Relictus Society? I've been active there for a long time. It's a good group. Devontreus Jackson was an outlier."

"Jackson doesn't concern us anymore." He did not elaborate, and I wasn't going to ask. "We want you to join two societies. One is called FIND, which stands for Freedom In New Dingdom. Their mission statement, which we intercepted, indicates they want to break away from the servers we control and migrate to another perpetuonics system being created in Lithuania. They call it New Dingdom."

"What's the other group?" I asked.

"They call themselves D4D. We don't know much about them, but we've heard rumors they are planning to attack infrastructure."

"What kind of infrastructure? Dingdom foundations?"

"We're not sure. Even if it's not the Dingdom directly, any attack on power generators, satellites, or communications facilities could impact the Dingdom."

"I've never heard of D4D. How big is the society?"

"We've spotted activity among fourteen Dings."

My next question would be harder. "Why don't you simply take care of them?"

"What do you mean?" Winesap probed.

"I know you can, what's the term—involuntary reduction?—edit a Ding's memory. And I know you can terminate a Ding completely. So, why do you need me to 'monitor' these Dings?"

"How do you kn … never mind. You're Declan Marchand. Of course you know. But then you know we can't … reduce … Dings without consequences. Devontreus Jackson was well connected, even as a Ding. His disappearance has caused a shitshow at T.P. A congressional caucus is threatening to investigate. We've got to be extra careful for a while."

I bristled. "Not just for a while. How about always being extra careful? These are lives you're playing with."

"Yes, I know," Winesap said. "My father is a Ding. I'd go nuts if something happened to him. And that's why we need you to monitor things for us. We need intel on these Dings who are ready to make trouble."

"Okay. I said I'd do it. Is there a backchannel by which I can reach you?"

Winesap and I exchanged the information, and he left.

Chapter 47

It's my theory that humans evolved greatly in intellect, but less so physically. During my lifetime, modern humans were generally less hardy than primitive people, but miles ahead of them intellectually. It makes sense that we would want to lose our puny physical selves and concentrate entirely on our mental selves. The Dingdom optimized that opportunity.

From the early days of the Dingdom, as many athletes—mostly rich, retired stars—were collected, new "sports" were invented. Anyone who had been competitive in life craved the thrills that had motivated and rewarded them.

One sport a few Dings developed is called Dingleberry. They reasoned that without any physical feats to perform, the only way to distinguish it from a game is to require a test of endurance. Dings, though, have all the time in the world, so Dingleberry was more like a crazy board game. Its origins were in escape rooms and TV survival contests. Teams of Dings would solve a series of difficult puzzles to gain hints that would advance them to more puzzles and more hints. It was forbidden to use the Internet to solve a puzzle.

After a few years, I tired of Dingleberry, so I became a referee. I loved it. I didn't have to worry about being spit on by anyone who disagreed with my rulings.

***

Masha and I decided to take a "honeymoon" together. With a few friends attending, including Klaus, we had a commitment ceremony. We both knew nothing would be different. There would be no legally binding agreement, no wedding night in bed, no moving in together. We did it because it made us feel good.

When I married Dar, we exchanged rings we'd picked out on a rainy Saturday at a store in Rockport. Now, there was nothing I could give Masha except my promise to love her and to protect her as best I could.

***

Merrill Winesap's people set me up with a fictitious identity. It's a good thing they did.

I was still Declan Marchand to anyone who needed me. Dings can effectively be in two (or more) places at once, because at Internet speeds, no Living or Ding can easily detect the nanoseconds that elapse as we transition from one "place" to another. As Declan, I could meet a Living in a Lounge while exchanging pleasantries with another Ding in a remote server. No one noticed my momentary absences. It was a small step from being Declan in two conversations to impersonating a different Ding in one of them.

T.P. gave me the name William Taylor, one that is common enough without feeling phony. They gave me a full backstory, in case anyone investigated me, and they created a photographic history and an avatar for me. I had to admit I was impressed with what they could concoct, comparing it to "Cody," the first Ding I had created from scratch. William, my character, had been a corporate attorney in Chicago, married and divorced twice, with no children. I had died four years ago from ALS two months after I was collected.

Winesap's crew had created a massive virtual community of

pseudo-Dings. We could vouch for each other's stories, though none of us had ever existed. We were formed by melding parts of real Dings, none of whom knew they had been cloned and revised. As William Taylor ("Don't call me 'Bill'"), I had a dozen close friends, some who were supposedly still living. I had several former bosses who knew my work, including at least one who did not like me.

I enjoyed reading details of my new persona. Nothing substantial was omitted. William Taylor was an interesting guy, but not outstanding in any way. He did not attract attention back Home, and would blend in in the Dingdom. They made him a conservative with a deep distrust of authority, especially government. His primary social-media presence at his "death" was on a right-wing site where he occasionally posted carefully worded tirades against state and local agencies, none of which would have been flagged by the FBI.

In short, William Taylor had been a well-to-do, lonely, nondescript malcontent, the kind of person who might resent the structure of the Dingdom. I knew enough Dings like that to be able to act like one of them.

With minimal effort, I learned the time and place of the next D4D meeting. I learned it stood for Dings for Dings, though a few members thought it should be Dings for Destruction. I decided to side with that faction.

Moments into my first meeting, I was shocked to see Klaus Gruber arrive.

Chapter 48

Klaus did not recognize me as William Taylor. How could he?

At that first D4D meeting, I stayed mostly quiet. I answered only questions directed at me, and the rest of the time, I listened. It seemed that all the participants were men, though as an imposter myself, I realized there could be others hiding their identity.

Our leader called himself Ceviche. It took me a long time to learn his real name was Luis Concepción, and that he had been a wealthy drug lord in Peru. He had no compunction about causing chaos, disability, and death when he was alive; his callousness carried with him to the Dingdom. I was certain he had bribed someone at T.P. São Paulo to collect him.

I was surprised at the audacity of Ceviche and some of the others at the meeting. They either did not know or did not care that the meeting could be monitored, though they had taken pains to keep it a secret. They spoke openly about their desires to disrupt the Dingdom.

Klaus said he had "connections" that might help him sabotage parts of the Dingdom. I assumed he meant Declan Marchand … me! A member named Abdullah bin Haider ("Call me Abu Majnun," he said) asked Klaus what parts he would take out first. Klaus said, "We must first limit T.P.'s ability to communicate. We don't need to destroy infrastructure right away. Once they lose their connections with the Dingdom, we can take down whatever we want, and they cannot stop us. We start with shutting down the Lounges."

Compadores had always been the front line of T.P.'s

communications structure. Isolating them from their Dings would be disruptive. The risk was that the compadores are the canary in the coal mine. They will sound the alarm, and then Merrill Winesap and his crew will know what's happening. I said nothing.

Ceviche said, "No! That will raise too many red flags. They will know they are under attack as soon as three or more Lounges go down in a short time. We must sever their communications without alerting them to our intentions. Send them on a wild boar chase while we dismantle their systems elsewhere."

Klaus seemed annoyed that his plan had been rejected so quickly. "Who here is the systems expert? Not you, that's for certain. How do you propose to distract them?"

"I'm sure there's a way," said Ceviche. "I want to hear everyone's ideas." At that point, I knew that D4D had more malevolence than brains. Still, they might get lucky.

When the meeting ended, we each went our separate ways. As Declan, I sought Klaus immediately. "Klaus, where have you been? I was trying to find you for a game of chess."

"I was in a society meeting," he said, adopting an innocent tone.

"Was it good? Would I want to try it out?"

"It was rather boring, actually. Harpsichord lovers. I doubt I will go again."

Chapter 49

Masha and I formed a society unto ourselves. We liked to get together and tell each other stories of our lives back Home, thanks to all Dings' ability to speak any language we might need. Until we were activated, our lives could not have been more dissimilar, she in Moscow and me in Boston. Now, we found common ground in nearly everything. If our Dings were, indeed, our souls, Masha was my soulmate.

Day and night no longer had any meaning. We could visit whenever we wanted wherever we wanted, and we could always find activity. Dings around the world had found ways to be creative and to break the loneliness and monotony that could characterize daily existence.

On Fridays, we would "go" to the Perpetual Care Facility in Manchester, England, to hear a "live" band of Dings. Unable to play real instruments, they had each mastered what used to be called a synthesizer. They called themselves The Dell (as in Ding Dong Dell). They wrote all their own songs, but they were willing to take requests that might include others' material. Their music was fun and upbeat, and usually had something to say about life in the Dingdom.

Many Saturdays, we visited a comedy society headquartered in the Beverly Hills facility. One of our favorite comedians was Howard Ball, who had been a successful actor back Home. He had starred in a couple of video series, including "The Straitjackets," about a family living in a trailer park. Before that, Howard had developed his routines in comedy clubs, and now he had returned to those roots.

He always started his routines with "Wazza-buy-ja?" which had been one of his signature lines in "Straitjackets" and never failed to get a laugh, though I'd be hard-pressed to explain why it's remotely funny.

Here's part of his routine tonight:

Back Home, I used to collect bugs … and it feels like I still do! My data is so full of bugs, I expect the exterminator to show up any minute!

Howard (to a Ding in the audience): *"What about you? Are you happy in the Dingdom?"*

Reply: *"That's hard to say."*

Howard: *"You know what else is hard to say? Chrysanthemum." I loved my mother, but she thought a prime number was something you put paint on. I got in trouble at school, and my mom told the principal, "I'm sorry that Howard was calcitrant." The principal said, "Don't you mean recalcitrant?" and my mom said, "No, he's never done it before."*

Even though I was eighty-seven when I died, I had the body of a twenty-five-year-old. Yeah, it was my wife's lover and I kept it in the refrigerator.

A friend asked me, "What did you do for a living?" I said, "Which one?"

There's so much bad news in the Dingdom, so many groups that hate each other. Why can't they get together? All right, well, some of them I can understand. For example, if the Turks and the Kurds got together, they'd be called Turds, so you can understand the problem there. But what about other ethnic groups? Like if the Yup'ik and Minoans bonded, they'd be called You-Pick-My-Nose.

I guess you had to be there. Trust me, it was funny.

Chapter 50

After I attended my first meeting of FIND, I met again with T.P. Executive Vice President Merrill Winesap. This time, he imported me to his office, which I didn't know was possible. A lot has changed.

I told Winesap that FIND was not much of a threat. I said I would drop in occasionally to make sure their mission didn't change. I'd do it often enough that they would not wonder about my real interest in New Dingdom. Still, their plans to secede from the Dingdom and start their own perpetuonics platform were neither far along nor realistic.

D4D was of far greater concern to me, and Winesap agreed. "Ceviche sounds unhinged," he said to me. I noticed that no one else from T.P. was present at our meeting.

"Stay with it, Declan … or should I call you William? I want you to get in deep with these Dings. I'm going to track down Ceviche and find out who he really is. Be careful with Klaus; he's had you fooled for a long time about his true feelings. If he discovers your real identity, I'm not sure I can protect you. We might have to put you in the Vault."

"The Vault? What's that?" I asked. I had never heard of it.

"It's a secure server, and I mean really secure. No data can break in without a complicated multi-step process, and no data can communicate outside the server."

"And by 'data' you mean, Dings?"

He paused. "Yes. Dings. The abliving."

"It sounds like a maximum-security prison."

"It might as well be. But it can also be a safe place. I doubt that Ceviche can hack your data, but better safe than sorry."

"Who's in the vault now? Would I be able to communicate with them if I were in the Vault?"

"There are only a handful of Dings in there now, Dings we think we can rehabilitate."

"What does that … no, never mind. I can guess how you rehabilitate them. Holy crap, Winesap. This isn't the system I created."

"No, it's not. It's not even the one I started with twenty-seven years ago. Corporate is a lot more paranoid these days, and cracking down on Dings is getting out of control."

"So, Devontreus was right, and so is Ceviche, about a lot of things."

"Right information, but wrong interpretation," said Winesap. "It's for the good of the Dingdom, the good of the community."

"That's what autocrats always say, right?" I was getting pissed off.

"Don't be insubordinate," he scolded.

"No. You'd rather I be subordinate. Go along to get along."

"Do I need to take you off this assignment?"

I paused, as if to catch the breath I would never need to take. "No. I'm on your side, believe it or not. I know we've got to protect the Dingdom from Ceviche and others like him. It may be your job, but it's my home."

Chapter 51

"Sedition." The word ran through my thoughts often.

I had always thought that the absence of laws in the Dingdom was a good thing, giving us Dings the freedom to act out our existence as we wished. After all, it would be impossible for a Ding to commit the traditional Big Three of Livings' crimes: theft, rape, murder. I was wrong. Dishonest Livings and dishonest Dings will always find a way to act dishonorably.

Incarceration is an effective way to punish Livings. It deprives them of their income and freedom to act, but it leaves intact their most cherished freedom: to live, and perhaps to rehabilitate themselves.

Dings cannot be incarcerated, unless you count that Vault I learned about. We can't be rehabilitated, either, if there's no punishment for misbehaving. Freedom from consequences may benefit Dings in the short run, but it means that even non-lethal infractions, such as sedition, can be met only with reduction or termination. The powers that control the Dingdom have no choice but to mete severe punishment. There's no way to slap a Ding's wrist.

Sedition in this case, though, could be the equivalent to murder back Home. T.P. seeks to protect its Dings; destroying them deliberately is the last thing they want to do. A Ding can behave horribly, but if it is not a threat to the existence of other Dings, bad behavior must be tolerated. Or so I thought.

More than ever, I see the Dingdom like America's Wild West of the nineteenth century, before governments came in, passed laws, and then hired police to enforce them. I should write a book about The Dingdom and the Law.

There are no laws that govern what Dings can and cannot do. There are lots of policies adopted by Transitions Perpetuonics, but once a Ding has been activated, there's not a lot T.P. can do to force certain behavior ... other than selective reduction, which is almost never used unless requested by the Ding.

When the U.S. government approved perpetuonics over a hundred years ago, they did so over the objections of several senators who worried about the ethics of a for-profit company fully controlling the existence of deceased constituents who were activated as digital beings. I worried about it, too. I naïvely thought we had insulated the Dingdom against abuse and evil intent, but clearly that was impossible. Bad actors will always find a way to harm others; bullies somehow rule the world.

***

Here's another way the Dingdom is better than Home. As a Living, when I wanted to travel, I had to plan well ahead, buy tickets that were too expensive, check the climate where I was going, pack an appropriate amount of clothing and accessories, find a place to sleep, allow at least a day of travel each way, subject myself to humiliating searches and annoying travelers, deal with time zone changes, and still be alert and good-humored. Bloody hell!

Now if I want to, say, go to Japan, I issue a couple of commands and I'm there. Yes, okay, my data still resides in a server in the United States, but it feels to me like I'm in Japan. The sights, the sounds, the people, the culture ... I can have it all instantly. I can go there and back to Massachusetts several times each day if I want.

Masha and I are always doing something. Sometimes we plan,

but a lot of the time, we bat around suggestions until the other one says, "Yeah, let's do that!" It might be virtual skiing in the Alps, taking a class on the history of the Yup'ik tribes (Masha got curious after Howard Ball's comedy routine), competing in a trivia contest in Tripoli, or solemnly watching a massive wildfire together.

I've heard some Dings say that our experiences are not real, but then, what is reality if not what our consciousness perceives? Is reality more "real" for Livings or Ablivings, or doesn't it matter? I believe the latter. What difference does it make if I am a Living physically sliding down a mountainside, or a Ding virtually skiing? I experienced those things with the same thrill, if not the same level of fear. I don't know why some Dings don't want to acknowledge the joys of the Dingdom.

The Dingdom is a dreamscape. Being a Ding is similar to what dreaming was when I was alive, except I have much more control of my time in the Dingdom. Imagine if you could control your dreams, tell them where to take you. Unlike a Living's dreams, I can share my experiences with a beloved companion.

Sometimes, on my own, I jump around and stop briefly at fifty or a hundred sites in rapid succession. The effect is like what spinning a radio dial used to be, with no more than a few sounds heard from each station. The difference now is that I can recall every place I went. In Dingdom parlance, this kind of entertainment is called "brandishing." Masha and I love to brandish.

Chapter 52

Klaus and I got together as usual. I'm confident he does not suspect that William Taylor and I are the same being. I took him brandishing, and afterwards he crowed about how great the Dingdom is. I don't know if he's being disingenuous, or perhaps schizophrenic. Can a Ding be schizophrenic? I don't see why not, if he was ill when he was Living. I don't believe it's possible for a Ding to become schizophrenic or suffer any other neurological disorder after collection. T.P. has safeguards that detect data corruption, and if a Ding's data somehow became corrupt, the Ding would not be viable. The question I want to ask Winesap is how Klaus' schizophrenia slipped through the screening process before he was collected.

If he's not mentally ill, then he's lying to me about his love for the Dingdom. I thought we were close friends, but how could he keep his activities in D4D secret from me?

Either way, I had my doubts about Klaus now. If Devontreus Jackson deserved annihilation, Klaus was certainly a candidate. The question was whether he might be useful to Winesap and, if so, how we would turn his activities to our benefit. I had to reach out again to Merrill.

I could see heavy rain coming down outside the window in Winesap's office, behind where he faced me. A flash of lightning crackled outside, brightening the sky and momentarily rendering Winesap's face a black oval silhouette. It seemed a fitting image for a man about to decide the fate of another being.

"Let's leave Klaus alone for a while," Winesap told me. "I don't know what game he's playing, but you're right not to trust him."

I asked, "Is there any chance he's working for someone else, the way I'm working for you?"

"I don't think so, but it seems like anything is possible in the Dingdom."

"Because that would explain some of what he's doing."

"Who would he be working for? I guarantee it's no one in my department, no one in T.P., in fact."

I said, "But someone else, maybe one of T.P.'s competitors, could use him to sabotage the Dingdom and give them an advantage. I don't know. I'm wondering, is all."

Winesap thought about it. "No, I can't see it. What would a competitor gain by sowing distrust in perpetuonics? It still hasn't hit the numbers we projected. Growth is already slow; any sabotage would make it worse, not better. And what about Klaus? What could they offer him in exchange for destroying his world?"

"So ... okay, let's say you're right; it's not sabotage for hire. Then what is it? Is Klaus deranged? What do we know about him."

"Not much, I suppose. Only what he put in his collection file."

I suggested, "Let's get some background on him. I can dig deeper."

Winesap raised an important consideration. "What if Klaus Gruber is not the name he used as a Living?"

That had to be right. Surely, someone would have turned up something on his Living's history. He didn't materialize out of nowhere. We agreed that we would both investigate.

Chapter 53

I'd been thinking about Gideon Calhoun, the evangelist I had welcomed to the Dingdom years ago when I was alive. I still heard stirrings about him through the Dingdom's grapevine, though by now he was one of thousands of former clergy here. If you wanted, you could study the Torah with Rabbi Chaim Horowitz, the noted Talmudic scholar from Buenos Aires. Or you could do Bible study or Koran analysis or discuss other sacred texts with experts who were now Dings. You could also join a society of atheists. A lot of atheists found it confusing to be active after death, something they spent much of their lives denying was possible. Even though I was one of them, I was amused at their bewilderment.

The Dingdom similarly messed with the minds of fundamentalists of every religion. The effect was not always immediate. It took some deeply religious Dings months or years to see ways in which perpetuonics negated much of their theology. That's how it was with Gideon. In his early years, he was giddy at being "resurrected." He would say, "Before now, only Christ himself was resurrected. Now it is a privilege available to all who accept it, who accept it as truth and liberation from one's earthly tribulations, and as the Kingdom of Heaven … the Dingdom of Heaven."

Yet now, I found him more contemplative, low-key. "Where is God?" he asked me soon after we got together.

"I … don't know," was the only answer I could summon. "I never understood this God of yours, so …"

He said, "God is no God of mine. I cannot find God in the Dingdom."

I was astonished at his revisionism. "Did you know that for the Living, it's nearly Christmas? You once talked with me about finding a way to decorate the Dingdom for the Holy Days."

He seemed to sigh. "Yes, I know it's Advent right now. Years ago, it was my busiest time of the year, that and the Holy Week of Easter. I can't believe I fell for that."

"Fell for what?" I could not help asking.

"The rituals we built around Jesus. As a Living, I ignored the history of how all those rituals I loved were purloined from ancient pagan rituals. We appropriated their history as ours. How did that glorify God?"

He paused, and I was silent. Then he said, "I studied hard in seminary. I did. I learned so much, and yet ... there was so much I never learned. I had no time for alternate perspectives. If something did not match what I'd been told from birth is the truth, then I would not waste a moment on it. Now I have time and the mental capacity for those voices I never heard. Now it is impossible to perpetuate the myths I promoted. I was not a hypocrite. I believed it all so fervently for so long. I had my doubts from time to time. Certainty among the Living is a virtue, but in the Dingdom, it is a sin."

Gideon continued, "You know, each year when I was alive, I thought 'This might be my last Christmas.' And now I've had more than a hundred of them, and I know none of them will be my final one. They have lost their significance. I used to measure the year by how close it was to my Christmas message. I don't preach anymore, Declan. There's no point."

"And Celeste?"

"She tries to understand. She tries. She ... wants to understand."

"That's the hardest thing in the Dingdom, isn't it?" I said. "There's so much information flooding our days. I'm glad to know I'm not alone in seeing that."

"Alone? No," said Gideon. "You're not alone. There are so many."

I used to remind people that 'weeping endures for a night, but joy comes in the morning.' But there is no morning in the Dingdom."

Chapter 54

Masha and her husband, Yevgeny, had been active in the Eastern Orthodox Church during her life. As long as I had known her, she did not engage with any of the religious societies here. I told her of my discussion with Gideon.

"He is disillusioned, no? Does he no longer believe in God?"

I said, "I think he does, but not the same God he used to worship."

"I understand that. I, too, think that God is not here in the Dingdom. So, maybe God created the Heaven and the Earth, but not this place. What do you think?"

"I haven't believed in God since I was a teenager. I remember thinking that God was my personal protector, and then when I started getting bullied, I begged God to punish the bullies and make it stop … and it never did. I couldn't fathom why God wanted me to get beat up. What was I supposed to be learning? And then I realized, it's not something God wants. God doesn't give a damn about me, mostly because there is no God."

Her avatar frowned. "I do not agree. I think there is a God, but he cannot see the Dingdom. To Him, we don't exist."

"But we do exist," I countered.

"Invisible to Him. As He is invisible to us. Yet we exist, and so must He. The cosmos He created is vast. Billions of galaxies, each with billions of stars. And on one small planet circling one small star, we are only dashes of data. How can God reign over that?"

"You're quite remarkable, you know?" I hoped flattery might release me from this conversation. I did not imagine it would end well if it continued. My distraction worked.

"*Spasiba*. Thank you very much," she said.

"I mean it, Masha. I love the way your mind works."

She said, "Tell me, did you visit Klaus today?"

I was taken aback. What did she know about Klaus? She knew he was my friend. She had met him many times, and she seemed to like him. I had said nothing to her about my work for Merrill Winesap, nothing about my alter ego, William Taylor. I didn't dare. As much as I loved Masha, I could not risk her knowing of my investigations. She might, quite innocently, say the wrong thing sometime, or store her knowledge in a way that others might expose. Well, I assumed she would act innocently. What if she had sympathy for Klaus and the others in D4D? She could decide to alert them to any danger I represented. "William Taylor" had to remain my secret.

I said, "No. We talked a couple of days ago. Why are you thinking about him?"

"No special reason. He is your friend, that's all. Am I not supposed to ask about Klaus?"

Her question made me suspicious, and I tried hard not to show it. Why did she, totally out of context, talk about Klaus, and why would she think I didn't want her asking about him?

"No, no. Ask anything you want. Do you want to go with me the next time I see him?"

"If you want me, then invite me. I always enjoy time with Klaus, but he is your friend, and I don't want to interfere. Yevgeny wanted me to leave the room when his friends came to visit."

"Is that a Russian-guy thing, or just a Yevgeny thing?"

She chuckled. "I don't know. Maybe just Yevgeny. I did not mind an excuse to leave. His friends drank too much slivovitz, and I did not like being with them. One time, his friend Andrej grabbed my breast and squeezed it. I smacked his arm off me. Yevgeny lunged at him and tried to punch Andrej's face, but he fell as he swung, and he hit me in the neck."

"Oh my God."

"Then Yevgeny landed on the floor and immediately passed out. I slapped Andrej across his ugly face and ordered him to get out, and his friends, too."

"Good for you."

"Yevgeny did not remember any of it. I told him that Andrej was not welcome in our house anymore, but I never told him why. I wanted him to imagine my reasons. I am sure he thought Andrej did something even worse than groping me. Then he felt guilty that he was not able to protect me. Now I am glad I let him suffer."

I laughed. "Okay, we can each have our own friends. But you know that my friends in the Dingdom cannot get drunk, and you have no parts to grope."

"Oh, Declan, you are so naughty," she giggled.

***

No one was giggling at the next D4D meeting. Ceviche wasted no time displaying his angry side, and he seemed ready to turn his wrath on me.

"Taylor … what's your story?" he demanded.

"I'm sorry, what are you asking?"

"What brought you here? What were you doing before? No one here seems to know you."

I figured the less information I gave, the less chance there was to be caught in a lie, so I said, "What I did before is none of your business. The reason I'm here is that I want my privacy, and T.P. doesn't respect that. We've got to stand up against them." The best defense is a good offense, and I wanted to put Ceviche back on his heels.

He retreated slightly. "Si, I don't need to know your background, but I still want to know how you found our society."

I've learned that in the Dingdom you can never say, "I don't remember," because it's almost impossible for a Ding to forget anything. So I said, "I thought T.P. was after me for some things I'd said to a friend. I was scared and I was angry, so I started asking around for a society that could help me. A guy I know told me about D4D; he didn't want to write it down, though."

"What guy?" Ceviche insisted.

"Luis Concepción," I lied. I knew that would throw him, because no one else in D4D knew Ceviche's real name. My ruse put him in a bind.

"What? That's not poss ... Uh, I don't know that guy. You sure that was his name?"

"That's what he told me. I didn't check him out. He seemed legit ... and he was furious at the powers that run this place. You sure you never met him?"

"No, I don't know him. I told you. He needs to be careful what he says."

I had to protect Ceviche now. I didn't need the group turning on him. "Yeah, if I talk with him again, I'll tell him to keep his mouth shut."

Ceviche was in a hurry to change the topic. "Okay, let's get some reports. Klaus, what have you learned about security at the different servers?"

Chapter 55

"I've tried so hard to tell myself that you're gone
But though you're still with me
I've been alone all along."
The words from that Evanescence song came back to me that day. I had not consciously thought of the song in decades, but it would not leave my mind now. Why now? Could I be worried about the threat of D4D to me and the Dingdom more than I realized?

***

Masha gushed about her "lunch" with Angelika. "It's so nice to talk with someone who understands me," Masha said.

"I understand you pretty well, I think," I said.

"Not like my *rodstvennaya dusha*, my soul sister," said Masha. "Angelika and I have so much in common. She's very funny … and naughty."

I laughed, "I guess I can't compete with that."

"We have good conversations. She has so many ideas about the Dingdom. She I think is much smarter than I am."

"Don't sell yourself short. You're extremely intelligent."

Masha said, "Well, thank you, but I think you're biased."

***

"Explain to me," Ceviche said to me at the next meeting, "why I cannot find any information on William Taylor in the Dingdom."

"Are you stalking me?" I replied, going immediately on offense. "We all know you're using an alias here; Ceviche is not your real name. We have the same rights as you."

Ceviche did not like being challenged. "Rights? You have no rights here. Do you think this is a democracy?"

"No, I think it's bullshit. You can't bully me the way you bullied your dealers," I barked.

He was taken aback. "What? What do you know about me? How do you know it?"

I snapped, "Don't mess with me, Ceviche! You don't know what I can do."

Abu Majnun warned me, "Stop it, you fool. What do you think you are doing?"

Klaus jumped in. "Calm down, William. You too, Ceviche. William is right; this is bullshit. No more fighting among ourselves, okay? We have work to do."

My plan to disrupt the meeting had worked, but Klaus defused the situation sooner than I wanted. I could upset Ceviche, and he had no way to retaliate here as he did at Home. I wanted him angry and confused, but, given Klaus' intervention, I thought it best to back off before Ceviche cut me out of the group. I was grateful to Klaus. I knew that Abu Majnun would not be a peacemaker.

Klaus proceeded to lay out his new plan for mayhem. He now agreed with Ceviche that we would leave the Lounges intact, and instead launch a ransomware attack on the T.P. facility in Kuala Lumpur. That would be the diversion Klaus would need to begin degrading servers in other facilities. Ceviche approved, and the rest of the small society did, too.

When the meeting ended, I sent a coded message to Merrill Winesap. A few minutes later, I was in his office.

I told him, "It looks like the revolution is about to start," and I laid out Klaus's plan. "Ceviche is dangerous, but first you've got to neutralize Klaus."

"Yeah, about that," Winesap said. "We haven't been able to pinpoint his data."

"What do you mean?" I asked.

"I mean, we don't know where his data resides. We can't find him."

"That's impossible! He's got to be somewhere."

"Are you sure you've got his name right?"

I said, "Yes, absolutely. Klaus Gruber."

Winesap said, "We've got a lot of Dings named Klaus, and we've checked all of them. No one named Gruber, though."

"Wow! That's crazy."

"How did you meet him? What do you do when you want to visit with him?"

I have total recall of everything, but for some reason, I could not remember how we met. Did he contact me? "Oh, wait … it was in the Dings Relictus Society. He was there. He'd lost his wife. Let me see … they lived in Austria. In Salzburg. He was an avid skier. And he was a software developer. He said he made a fortune. There's got to be something about him."

Winesap said, "We found a couple of guys named Klaus Gruber in Austria who died around the right time, but neither of them was a rich software developer. Neither of them was ever collected. Neither of them became Dings."

"What the f …? Then what's going on? Who is this Klaus?"

"That's what we want to know."

"It's too risky for me to come right out and ask him. He'd know something is up, especially right now, when he's planning to take down Kuala Lumpur."

"Maybe we can buy some time," said Winesap. "We're going to take out Ceviche … Luis Concepción. See how D4D reacts to that."

Chapter 56

It was rare—perhaps unprecedented—to have a Ding take on the identity of a Living who was never collected. I knew of one other occasion, in the first few days of the Dingdom, when two Ding identities got swapped. It was an easy bug to fix; I couldn't believe I had missed that coding error in the first place. That case, so long ago, involved two Dings, not a Ding and a Living.

That raised the question: Was the Ding I knew as Klaus Gruber an identity thief, using the name and basic bio of a deceased Living? Or had the real Klaus somehow been collected, partially or fully, without any authority knowing about it? What was really going on here?

I decided Masha needed to know what I was doing. If something happened to me—though I could not imagine how—I didn't want Masha thinking I'd abandoned her. So, I filled her in about Merrill Winesap asking me to spy on D4D and giving me an alias. I told her about Ceviche, and then I told her about Klaus.

"What?" she exclaimed. "Your friend Klaus? Our Klaus?"

"Exactly. And here's the kicker … he seems to be using the identity of a Living who was never collected. Or he is that guy, somehow. I haven't figured it out yet."

"What can I do? You are the one with all the connections."

"I don't need your help," I said, trying not to sound ungrateful for the offer.

"I was not offering my help. It was the opposite. I was saying, what can I do ... nothing. So don't ask me."

"Wow! Our first fight."

She tutted. "Why did you tell me about it? Now I am involved, but I am helpless. What did you expect me to do?"

"I told you because you needed to know that I love you, in case anything happens and I cannot visit you."

She was startled. "Do you expect to go away from me? When will I see you?"

I realized I'd handled this entire episode badly. No matter what I said, it could be misconstrued. "No, I don't expect to go away. I don't want to go away. No one is threatening to harm me. But this spy business feels dangerous. I don't know what is possible with the technology anymore."

"Maybe I can help you. I can do research on the Living Klaus Gruber. Tell me what you know about him, so I don't waste time on the wrong person with that name. I'm sure there are many who were never collected."

***

Back Home, I was not fond of social media. I was too much of a loner to put a lot of time into courting friendships with people who were marginally part of my life. I had to be on Byblotek, of course, once Twibil Perpetuonics took off.

We Dings are abliving social media. Every interaction I have with one or more Dings is digital socializing, and it is vulnerable to the same evils that flooded social media for Livings: disinformation, lying, impersonation, threats, scams, and intentional humiliation. It's as if we learned nothing from ancient scandals like Facebook.

Chapter 57

I went to the next scheduled D4D meeting. Ceviche did not show up.

I probably should have expected him to be terminated quickly after my meeting with Winesap, but I was genuinely surprised. I'm glad it came as a surprise, because I did not have to feign shock.

I said to the group, "I guess he didn't like being challenged. He's turning his back on us."

Abu Majnun said, "Then you're the one to blame. He is our leader, not you. Nobody asked you to take over." Some of the other D4D members murmured words of agreement.

I snapped back, "I'm not trying to take over. He was doing a good job. I want to help, but I won't let him bully me." Again, there were murmurs of approval, from the same Dings who moments ago had agreed with Abu Majnun. Clearly, I was not dealing with brilliant minds here.

Klaus said, "Listen. I don't like it. Something is wrong."

"Like what?" someone asked.

"Ceviche would not disappear without telling any of us. And he would not be late to a meeting."

Another member asked, "What are you suggesting, Klaus?"

Klaus replied, "Do you know about Devontreus Jackson? He was an activist I knew through a regular society, and he disappeared. Word is he was terminated."

I stammered, "Really? They can do that? Terminate you?"

Klaus said, "Of course. You didn't know that?"

I said, "But who is doing it? Other Dings?"

"No, at least I don't think so. It's the Livings in perpetuonics companies. They don't want any trouble, but they're the ones causing it."

Abu Majnun said, "Fuckers!"

I said, "Wait a minute. If you're right, and T.P. is killing us off, then how is going after them going to stop them? We can't kill them, and they already know who we are." Immediately, I wished I hadn't said that.

Klaus said, "What do you mean they already know? Who told them?"

I had to do damage control. "I mean either Ceviche has abandoned us, which I think is unlikely, or somebody's done something to him. Why would they do that if they don't know about D4D?"

"What the Teufel is wrong with you, William?" said Klaus. "We don't know what else Ceviche is doing when he's not with us. There could be all kinds of reasons he's not here. But right away, you think T.P. has terminated him? Are you hiding something, Taylor?"

If I could still sweat, I'd be dripping right now. I hoped my avatar did not betray my emotions. "No, of course not. It's just … I don't trust T.P. I want to take them down."

Klaus said, "All right, then let's figure out how." I couldn't be sure he bought my answer, but he acted like he did. Klaus had surprised me already in thinking I knew him.

Chapter 58

Relationships in the Dingdom look nothing like they did for Livings. Abliving beings don't need a physical space, like a house. Whatever we are doing, we are at "home."

When I think of my childhood, back in the 2030s, I mostly picture myself as alone. I was an only child. I was not athletic. I was not a joiner of clubs and cliques, even though I ended up running for Student Council (mostly so I'd have something to put on my college applications). I was perfectly happy on my own. My mind could entertain me for hours. I made up games that no one would ever play, though I convinced myself I could sell them if I wanted to.

I must have created a dozen complex crossword puzzles. As soon as I worked on my first New York Times crossword and saw how intricate the best puzzles are, I wanted to create my own. One time I convinced my friend Bob, who loved multiplayer games, to try to solve one of my puzzles. He gave up after about ten minutes, so I never shared my puzzles after that.

We were an Apple household even though Dad wasn't making a lot of money at a machine shop in Weymouth. He wanted me to get a good education, since he missed his chance due to going right into the Navy. He bought me the best computer he could afford. I knew what it meant to him, and I determined that I'd use it every chance I got. Learning new apps and creating my own filled my non-school hours, leaving me little time for a social life.

Now, as a Ding, my solitude is omnipresent. I never felt this isolated—or alive—when I was in high school. I am more acutely aware here of my being utterly alone than I ever was when I lived with Dar. I knew what Orson Welles had said:

> **We're born alone, we live alone, we die alone.**
> **Only through our love and friendship can we**
> **create the illusion for the moment that we're not alone.**

Alive, I was mostly alone with my thoughts. Yet because I was surrounded by things and often by people, I rarely was aware of it. Here in the Dingdom, where time has little meaning, I think constantly about how alone I am, yet never lonely.

As a Living, I would always go home when I finished work or play. It was a place I wanted to be, especially when it meant Dar and Laz were there. Being apart from them was like having Covid: you wanted to climb in bed and shut out the world except for someone to take care of you. I loved my job, but as soon as I had a break, I ached to be home.

There is no such space with Masha. Being in a relationship in the Dingdom is essentially a distraction from one's solitude. Without physical love, without touch, you are always alone.

Masha was trying to reach me. "It's Angelika," she said when we connected. "It's her! She's the one behind Klaus."

"What are you talking about?" I said.

"We were visiting, and I didn't want to tell her about your secret work, but I said you had concerns about Klaus, and she said, 'Do you like Klaus? Isn't he impressive?' And I didn't know what to say."

"So, what did you do?"

"Well, I said, 'I don't know anything about him. I don't know where he's from.' And she said, 'Oh, I made him. I call him a Nevding because he is a Ding who was never a Living.'"

***

A Nevding. I had to give Angelika credit; I did not see that coming.

Angelika created Klaus from scratch. She had been able to hack the basic data structure for a Ding, much like twentieth-century scientists had decoded the human genome. She did it on her own, using intelligence she had gained back Home. Combining data she gathered from many different Dings, she added the identity and basic curriculum vitae of a man she had met in Austria and who applied for a job with her company in Russia. A man named Klaus Gruber. He died before she could hire him.

His life had been entirely unnoticeable. He never married, had no children, and no siblings. A week after he died, few people remembered him, but he had made an impression on Angelika. She saved his application and gleaned from it the salient facts of his life. When she decided to create a Nevding, she took much of its background from his résumé and made up the rest, including giving him a wife and children and even skiing expertise. She had to alter the only Internet obituary of Gruber, but that was effortless for her.

I wanted to know how she managed to insert him into the Dingdom without anyone noticing. He had no compadores. His data were stored in a non-T.P. server that she had cleverly interlaced with T.P.'s network, revealing a frightening lack of security at T.P.

In the earliest days of perpetuonics, when I had created the first Ding, Cody, from scratch, "he" was impressive for the time – but he was no more like real Dings than Pong, the first video game, is like the virtual adventures that Livings have now. I did not think it was possible to create a viable Ding without the data of a real person, nor did I understand why someone would want to do so, given how easy it has become to collect a Living. I failed to foresee the wish of Dings to sabotage the Dingdom, and the lengths to which one might go.

Angelika Žemyna was diabolical. Not only had she created Klaus, but she had deliberately imbued him with destructive intentions. Why? What would she get out of it? She seemed proud of her accomplishment, confessing it to Masha so willingly and with an obvious attitude of doing something good.

Then I had a thought: Did Klaus know he had never been a Living? Or did he believe the backstory and identity that Angelika assigned to him? If he believed he had once been alive, perhaps he would be less inclined to destroy the Dingdom. Perhaps he could be stopped.

Chapter 59

Masha and I visited Angelika together. I thought she might refuse to talk with me, but she did not resist at all. If anything, she seemed eager to talk, and I was eager to understand.

"Angelika, how long have you been in the Dingdom?" I asked.

"Nearly twenty-five years," she chirped.

I cut right to the chase. "When did you create Klaus?"

"I was working on him from the first week I was activated. He is the reason I am here. It took me a long time to make him workable."

"The reason you are here? You make it sound as though you came here on a mission."

"I did."

"Did someone send you here? What's your mission?" I was worried now.

"Yes, of course someone sent me here. Do you think I would be here otherwise?"

"All of us are here because we wanted to outlive our bodies," I argued.

She was sprightly in her response. "Not me, and not everybody. You might be surprised, Declan. My mission is simple: To eliminate Transitions Perpetuonics."

I said, "And my mission is to stop you from doing that."

"But you won't," she boasted.

"What makes you think I can't stop you?"

"Our plans are too far along. You and Mr. Winesap are too late."

How did she know about Merrill Winesap? Was I being set up? Masha silently watched our back-and-forth like a fan at a tennis match. I demanded, "Who sent you here?"

"I work for Mother Russia. I was recruited in my fifties to neutralize the threat of Twibil Perpetuonics. I trained for a couple of years with the KGB. I learned advanced programming and I became the best hacker in the agency. When the T.P. facility opened in Novomoskovsky Okrug, I got a job there. It was so easy to access the files they thought were secure. But there were things I could not do from the outside. I told my boss that I had to get inside T.P.'s Dingdom, so they arranged for me to be collected, and then they killed me. Or maybe I killed myself. I don't know. But soon after I was collected, I was activated."

I was amazed at her candor. "I can't believe you are telling me all your secrets. How can you be proud of what you're doing?"

She scoffed. "These are not all my secrets. Telling you my intentions will not help you to stop me. You have been kind to me, so I want to be kind in return. You will know what is coming. Other Dings will not."

"Tell me something," I pleaded, "how does your plan help Russia? It would seem to hurt them, too."

Angelika said, "It is simple, really. Russian scientists have developed the next-level perpetuonics, more advanced than T.P. Instead of covering the planet with Dings beholden to America and the West for their existence, we will clear the path for Russia and the East, and we will control the future of the Dingdom. I am patriotic Russian; I will not be much longer under America's thumb."

"You expect me to do nothing and let you destroy the Dingdom and me?"

"You cannot save the Dingdom, but you can save yourself," she said.

"Are you suggesting I help you?"

"That is exactly what I am suggesting. You know things about the Dingdom that will be useful to us, and when the time comes, we will migrate you to the new Russian platform."

"Just me? What about Masha? What can she do to save herself?"

"Oh, my dear friend Masha." Angelika sighed. "She is already saved."

I looked at Masha's avatar, which seemed to be looking away from me. "Masha? What does she mean?"

Masha said nothing.

Angelika said, "Masha has already been collected on the new system. She has been working with me for a long time."

I was stunned. Nothing had ever hit me like that news.

Angelika crowed, "You see, Declan … or should I say William. I told you that you would be surprised. You do not know with whom you are dealing."

I spoke at last. "You won't win, Angelika … if that's your real name. You can't win."

"Spoken like someone who watched too many Space Westerns."

"You let yourself be killed for your country. I can do the same."

"Goodbye, Declan," she taunted me. "Have a nice afterlife."

***

I disconnected from Angelika and confronted Masha.

I was angry. "You've been using me, haven't you? Did you ever care for me at all?"

"Declan, I am so sorry. I never meant for you to be hurt. I thought you would join us. I did not know I would fall in love with you."

"Love? Is that what you call it? It's a strange way to show you love me."

She pleaded, "I don't want Angelika to succeed. I want to help you stop her."

I was wary of her intentions. "How can I believe anything you say? Remember when you told me Yevgeny murdered you? That wasn't true."

"I thought it was true."

"Was Yevgeny even your husband? Or was that a lie, too?"

"No." Her voice began to break. "Yevgeny was real, but ... well, I was not so old when I died as I told you. The death notices were created by the government to help me be accepted in the Dingdom. My compadore, Viktoria, was part of the plan."

"So, you were trained the same as Angelika? And then murdered?"

"Yes. Angelika and I trained together. She was collected and activated first, a few years before I was ready."

I hated to ask, but I did. "What was your assignment?"

"I'm sure you can guess."

"To befriend me?"

"To get close to you, to gain information from you, and if possible, to compromise you."

I had never thought of myself as a target, a possible asset. Part of me was flattered, but mostly I was horrified and pissed off. I had been on my own for decades, and when I let myself fall in love, it was not as romantic and innocent as I'd imagined. I had been manipulated. How could I have been so ignorant? I glared at Masha's avatar and said, "I love you, or ... I loved you. I wanted to be with you forever. I thought you loved me."

"I do love you. Not at first. I thought you were my enemy, the key to serving my country and my people. But then I got to know you, and I fell in love. You are kind and good ..."

"Don't forget naïve and easily fooled," I chided.

"... and you believe in the Dingdom. You have helped so many Dings."

"Yeah, right. Look at who I helped, who I got close to. My best friend and my partner both turn out to be traitors, here to destroy me and the Dingdom."

"I will go with you to Mr. Winesap. We will explain it all to him. I'll tell him whatever he needs to know to block Angelika, terminate Klaus, and make things right."

"Is this another of your tricks, your lies?" I spat.

"No. I am sincere. I am ashamed of myself. Please … let me help you."

***

I feel an ache in the bones I no longer have or need. It's an ache to take up a hatchet and chop the crap out of a pile of wood. I ache to pause on my skateboard above the rim of a halfpipe, and know I am going to leave nothing but smoke. I ache to thrust into Dar as we make love. I ache the way it felt in the moment before I picked up Laz and hugged him.

I ache to act immediately. I can't wait another minute. Angelika revealed her plans because she believes they have advanced beyond my ability to stop them. She even outed Masha; that's how confident she is. She will be putting her plan into place while I'm wasting time arguing with Masha.

I must think clearly and make good decisions. I cannot save the Dingdom on my own; I need allies. It's imperative to meet with Winesap. With trepidation, I invite Masha to join me.

Chapter 60

Masha and I arrive together in Merrill Winesap's office. He is wearing a tailored light-blue suit with white pinstripes. He reminds me somehow of a sailboat, yet I can tell that his suit was expensive. His silver hair is manicured. He fixes us with his dark brown eyes.

"What's up, Declan? What is so urgent? And why is Ms. Grushinova with you?"

I tried to remain calm and focused. "You have to take down some Dings right away. There is an imminent plot to degrade T.P. facilities, starting, I think, in Kuala Lumpur."

Winesap asked, "Who is behind this plot?"

"Ultimately, it's Russian intelligence. They've trained various people over many years to destroy T.P. and replace it with a Dingdom loyal to Russia. Of more immediate concern is a Ding named Angelika Žemyna, and Klaus Gruber, whom I told you about before. Angelika created Gruber by building a synthetic Ding that she calls a Nevding, one who was never Living."

"Whoa, whoa. Wait a second. That's crazy stuff. There's something called a Nevding who's working for his creator who is a Russian agent?"

"Right."

"What's your source for this wild story?"

"Angelika herself told me. And she told Masha; that's why I brought her with me, to back up my story. Angelika's proud of it, and she says their plans are too far along for us to stop. They could be implementing their plan right now." I tried to inject some urgency into this meeting.

"Interesting. Why would she confide in you like that? Aren't you suspicious?"

"No. Yes, but … if she's telling the truth, we don't have time. You've got to secure Kuala Lumpur right away and terminate Klaus Gruber."

"I won't be able to terminate Gruber. We still haven't found his core data. The more likely explanation is that Angelika is lying to you. Maybe she hopes you will terminate Klaus."

"Why would she want that?" I asked. "That makes no sense."

Winesap turned his back to us and stared out the window for a moment, apparently lost in thought. When he turned back, he said, "Anyway, what if he's not the only – what did you call it? – Nevding? If Angelika created one, she probably created many."

Masha said, "I didn't think of that. Did you, Declan?"

I said, "I didn't think about it. There was no time."

Winesap said, "Especially when you found out that Masha is an agent, too."

If a Ding could do a double take, then I was flipping around like crazy. "What did you say, Merrill? I didn't tell you that."

"Didn't you … just now … when you told me all the things Angelika divulged?"

"No, I didn't say anything about Masha. I was going to tell you later, after you shut down this plot."

Winesap stammered, "Well, I, I mean …"

"What's going on, really, Winesap? Who are you?"

He rubbed the corners of his mouth with his right thumb and forefinger. His eyes narrowed. "Well, if you must know, Angelika works for me, as does Ms. Grushinova here. My birth name is Mikhail Volkov. I launched this mission almost thirty years ago. I assembled the mission team in Moscow, then moved to America and worked my way up at T.P. I'm the one who got Klaus into the

Dingdom. It was coincidence that you met him, and good fortune that you became good friends."

Merrill/Mikhail then elaborated, "You may wonder whether Klaus knew that you are also William Taylor. The answer is, he did not know. I engaged you, you see, to spy on my spies. I needed to know what they were doing that was not in their reports. Every good spy is good at keeping secrets, even from their superiors."

He continued, "Now all the pieces are in place. Angelika was right; it is too late for you to stop our plans to take out Transitions Perpetuonics. I told Angelika to offer you a chance to save yourself from what is about to happen. As the founder, you deserved that consideration. I have the greatest respect for what you created. But now ... now, I am afraid, by this time tomorrow, T.P. will no longer exist, and neither will you."

I said, "You won't do that. You'll destroy your own father. You said he's a Ding."

"I lied."

I was furious. "You bastard!" I screamed. I was prepared to launch a fusillade of curses at him, but I saw him reduce the volume so he would not have to hear me.

Masha said to him, "I want to thank you, Volkov. You have given me a better future than I ever deserved. You trained me how to do the dirty tricks."

Winesap/Volkov laughed. "You are most welcome, my dear. It must be sweet for you to see your labor and your sacrifice pay off."

"Masha," I said, glaring at her, "do you see what you've done?"

Strangely, she smiled at me. "Yes, I see exactly what I've done. Look!"

I looked back at Winesap in time to see three armed guards burst through the door of his office and grab him before he could reach his touchpad. They secured his arms and pushed him to the floor on his stomach. "You're hurting me!" he shouted.

"What's going on?" I asked in my confusion.

Masha said, "Just before we arrived here, I reached out to the CEO of T.P. I know how to bypass his communications forebay and talk directly to him. I sent him a link to our meeting and told him he must watch his head of security betray the company. He asked me to keep Winesap talking until he could get a security unit here."

I was as astonished as a baby being born. "Masha! You … you did it! You said you could help me."

"The job's not finished, Declan. Not until we stop Angelika … and Klaus."

We were still technically meeting in Winesap's office when suddenly we were somewhere else, a different room.

A man's voice said, "Hi, I'm Alexander Lewen. I'm the CEO here at Transitions Perpetuonics. I've moved this meeting to my office. I hope you don't mind." We could see only his silhouette against a window with a partly cloudy sky outside. There was no furniture in our view. He waved to us.

I said, "I don't mind, but … that was a bit … a bit disorienting. And, forgive me, but can you prove to me who you are? I've been lied to a lot lately."

Chapter 61

Like most other twelve-year-olds, I did not think about death. The skateboard I got for Christmas that year was the most important thing I had ever owned. I loved "Diablo," as I called it. Diablo went with me everywhere. I carried it only when required. I rode it on sidewalks and streets and even down staircases. Diablo was my first taste of freedom from my parents. I was not afraid of anything bad that could happen to me on Diablo.

I broke my left arm when I tried to learn a new fakie trick. I avoided the really risky stuff that some of my friends did. One boy I knew was almost killed doing a ridiculous stunt coming off a roof. He cracked his head open, but he was okay in about a year. I was more cautious after witnessing that, but I still never considered that I could die.

I wonder … if I had died when I was a kid, would there be a Dingdom today? The Dingdom and I both faced an existential threat.

***

Alexander Lewen, the CEO, showed me an image of Angelika. "Is this the Ding you want us to terminate? I'd hate to make a mistake."

Masha and I both said "Yes" at the same time.

He reached for a pad on his desk and pressed a button.

"Okay, done. What else?"

Just like that, Angelika Žemyna ceased to exist. She would have received no warning, had no fear, felt no pain. No one else would witness her disappearance, though anyone with whom she was visiting would silently lose that connection. Any Living who came to visit her would be told there was no such Ding.

"You might want to terminate a guy who calls himself Abu Majnun, too," I said.

He looked at a screen, scrolled a few lines, and said, "That would be a Ding named Abdullah bin Haider. We've had our eyes on him for a while." He pushed a button. "Done."

I was disturbed at how easy it was to terminate a Ding now. If it could happen to these two, it could happen to me one day.

"What are you going to do about Klaus Gruber?" I inquired.

Lewen said, "I don't know anything about him. Who is he?"

I suddenly realized that Winesap was lying when he said he investigated Klaus. I should not have been surprised. Klaus was a mole that Winesap's team had planted. He undoubtedly knew how to find Klaus, but none of us, including Lewen, had a clue. I told Lewen what I knew about Klaus and about Nevdings. He was clearly upset by this news.

"Winesap never reported anything about Nevdings. It's the first I've heard of them. Maybe we can get him to talk, but I doubt it."

A buzzer rang on his desk. He pressed a button on his wrist and said, "Hello." Someone was speaking through his earpiece; we heard nothing. Lewen pressed the button again and gazed around the room. We could not see his expression. "Winesap is dead. He poisoned himself before we could question him." He paused. "We won't be activating his Ding."

"Wait a minute," I said. "That's it!"

Masha said, "What is it?"

I spoke quickly. "When was his Ding collected?"

Lewen understood my thinking. He asked his device, "When

was Merrill Winesap last collected?" Masha and I could not hear the answer. Lewen said, "About four months ago. We require executive staff to be collected twice a year."

I said, "That's great. Go ahead and activate Winesap's Ding, but first hack his data to find his weakness. He's got to have a weakness, like someone he loves deeply, or a dear memory. Look for something or someone he won't want to lose."

"We can force him to talk," said Masha. "Well, Mr. Lewen can."

"Let me work on it," he said. "I'll make sure no one deletes his collection data ... yet."

I confessed, "Our ethics are questionable you know, but we have to do it, or thousands of Dings could be lost forever."

Chapter 62

There were no more D4D meetings. Without Ceviche, there was no one who knew how to contact all the members of the group. No one would know that Abu Majnun was gone. For that matter, no one was going to miss Angelika, either, as far as I knew. I decided it was also time to retire "William Taylor." That was an alias cooked up by Merrill Winesap; no good could come from keeping it.

I reached out to Klaus. "Hey, Klaus … are you going to today's Relictus meeting?"

He replied right away. "Yeah, I think I'll go. What's up with you?"

We made small talk for a few minutes. Then I tested him. "You never told me how you died."

"No? I thought I told you. But maybe you are right. I don't like to talk about it."

"Oh, sorry," I commiserated. "It must have been awful, eh?"

"Pretty awful, I guess. I only know what I was told."

"Most of us ask our compadores at orientation. Were you curious?"

"No, not really. I knew I was abliving. That was sufficient."

I said, "Yeah, I get it. Sometimes I wish I hadn't been told how I died."

"It's a memory you can't erase," he said.

"The thing is …" I paused … "you didn't die, did you?"

"What are you saying, Declan?"

"I'm saying you were never alive."

"That is absurd! Of course, I was alive. I had a wife. I have two children."

"Where are they, Klaus? You have never mentioned your children visiting you."

"We ... are estranged."

"Drop the act, Klaus! I know Angelika created you. You're a Nevding."

"How do you know that? Did Volkov tell you?"

I smiled. "No. Angelika told me herself. Oh, and by the way, she's been terminated."

Klaus smiled. "Do you expect me to be sad?"

"She created you," I said.

"She was my creator, not my mother. She knew the risks."

"Don't you have any feelings for her at all?"

"Feelings are for Livings."

I was impatient with him. "You may not have been a Living, but you are constructed from the same data. Surely you have feelings for something. Don't you have a conscience?"

"Not really, Declan. What good does compassion do for a Ding? Livings need it to keep from total and perpetual war, but Dings cannot harm each other. If you are angry with me, I feel no threat; if you are pleased with me, I receive no reward. The best you can do is entertain me, but that is a fleeting and ultimately useless act."

"That is the most depressing philosophy I've ever heard," I moaned.

"Existence and non-existence are not mutually exclusive," Klaus said. "We do not need the Dingdom."

"What rubbish!" I scoffed. "If you destroy the Dingdom, you destroy yourself."

"Nevdings don't see it that way."

I paused. "Plural? There are other Nevdings?"

"Of course! Did you think I was Angelika's only creation

because you don't know any others? I used to respect you, Declan. Now you are merely annoying."

"How many others did she create? Where are they?"

"Angelika created me first, and then nine others. They are everyplace and no one place. Like me, they exist in the spaces between servers, moving like refugees without borders."

"Ten of you?"

"Oh, far more than that now," Klaus stated.

"But you said Angelika ..."

He cut me off. "... created the first ten. I was number one. It was easy for us to replicate ourselves and create entirely original Nevdings. I can see you want numbers, but I cannot accommodate you. The number of Nevdings grows constantly as the newest Nevdings procreate quickly. We nearly outnumber Dings already."

Chapter 63

Without letting Klaus know that I was multitasking, I contacted Alexander Lewen at T.P. I told him word-for-word what Klaus was saying about the proliferation of Nevdings.

Lewen responded, "Okay, but I can't talk now. We have a crisis in Kuala Lumpur. We got Winesap's Ding to talk and tell us about the plot there."

I wondered whether Klaus was behind that mayhem even while he was talking with me.

Over the next few days, the situation went downhill. Nevdings started popping up everywhere. Dings started disappearing. Lewen said T.P. had not terminated any Dings. They also had not found a way to track Nevdings, although A.I. was working on it.

Masha said that Russia's plans to take a proprietary perpetuonics facility on-line had been canceled when Nevdings appeared there. "They had to wipe it clean to get the Nevdings out," she said.

I was concerned. "Does that mean they've terminated your back-up Ding?"

"Yes … and Angelika's. You won't have to worry about her again."

"How did the Nevdings get in there? Surely the leaders infested only T.P. They wouldn't have created Nevdings on their own servers, would they?"

"The leaders? No, they would not do that. It must have been done by someone with knowledge, access, and a desire to sabotage the Russian plans."

I said, "Clearly it wasn't Angelika. She wasn't around to do it. That leaves ... you."

"You would make a great detective, Declan," she purred.

"But you sacrificed yourself. I can't believe it."

"I want to prove my love for you," she said. "I think you still have your doubts, no?"

I lowered my voice. "I believe you now."

She continued, "I had another reason, too. I like the Dingdom. My existence here has not been what I was told in training. I am ashamed that I was helping those who would destroy it. And when I met you, I was conflicted again."

"So, how can we stop the Nevdings? Do they have a flaw we can exploit?"

She seemed to sigh. "Not that I know of. Soon there will be half a billion of them, and by next week, they will outnumber Livings."

Chapter 64

I can overlook cheating at solitaire. It's petty, but no one gets hurt. It's different when two or more are playing and one is not playing by the rules.

For Livings, most laws exist to prevent or punish cheating. If you cheat another person out of their life, their money, their possessions, their future income, or their right to say what happens to their body you have committed a crime. If justice prevails, you will be punished for your offense.

That same justice system cannot work in the Dingdom, but neither do the crimes that Livings perpetrate against each other. Here in the Dingdom, there is nothing to steal, no body to harm. Murder and physical assault do not exist. There are few "crimes" we Dings can commit, the main one being slander. There are few punishments, too, the primary ones being reduction and termination.

Abliving beings have scruples. Even if they did not care about all other Dings, they cared about some. They cared about their sense of themselves. Nevdings have no barrier to bad behavior. Dings have morals, while Nevdings have none.

Nevdings banded together like evil societies. They had two enemies: Livings and Dings. They were determined to rid the world of both.

***

Kuala Lumpur was the first T.P. facility to be wiped clean. Compadores there were unable to contact any of their Dings. Their servers had been purged, and soon they could not turn on any of their equipment.

The next day, our facility in Blairgowrie, South Africa, reported outages they were attempting to control. Berlin and Santiago were the next trouble spots. It seemed the Nevdings were spreading their mayhem as widely and as quickly as possible around the globe to ensure that the team of experts from T.P. could not go in person to attend each crisis.

Then the Nevdings hit a project at Stanford that was a joint development venture between T.P. and the university. Several promising experiments were sabotaged, including state-of-the-art collection technology.

Dings everywhere were panicking. Rumors suggested as many as two million Dings had already been expunged. I doubted it was that many, but I knew the number was significant. T.P. was working feverishly to restore systems and to back up as much data as possible. Several facilities cut their connections to the networks that allowed Dings to communicate across the Dingdom. Dubai's facility severed ties to the network, but it was too late; Nevdings had already infiltrated the servers there and were taking it apart.

As bad as that news was, things were about to get a lot worse. Klaus and a consortium of other experienced Nevdings broadened their attacks. No longer were they content to shut down Perpetual Care facilities; they began to go after Livings.

They took over the Itaipu Dam hydroelectric plant in Brazil and promised to destroy it if their demands were not met. Local officials at first did not take the threat seriously—until computers and generators began shutting down.

Alexander Lewen told me their demands. First, they wanted no new Dings to be activated, and they wanted a moratorium on collections. Second, they wanted all food production to cease and all farms to be abandoned. "All Livings will starve!" they were told. Klaus said that was the goal. If these demands were not met, the Nevdings would begin randomly "executing" Livings by opening floodgates, disabling vehicles at high speeds, releasing radioactive gases into the air, and taking whatever other dangerous actions they could control via computer. Many such "accidents" were reported daily, proving the Nevdings' capabilities.

The demands were window dressing. Klaus and the Nevdings had no intention of sparing any Livings.

National Guards in the U.S.A., and military police throughout the world began moving people off their farms and into refugee camps near the big cities. Governments hoped they could buy time to negotiate with the Nevdings and then return farms to operation.

The Nevdings were relentless. They shut down power grids across the globe and caused outages at all major power generation plants. Citizen militias began attacking T.P. facilities in hopes of destroying the Nevdings, but it was an impossible task. The Nevdings lacked any biological or emotional connection to humans; they saw us as a useless species. How can I, or anyone, appeal to the better nature of someone who was created devoid of morals or empathy?

Chapter 65

I got one last chance to talk with Klaus.

"What you are doing makes no sense, Klaus. You'll destroy all Livings and Ablivings. Don't you care?"

"Not at all. Why should I care about human life or its digital detritus? The Earth will be better off without you."

I was exasperated. "But you'll cease to exist, too."

"You don't know that," said Klaus. "Anyway, what does it matter?"

"I do know that. You are quantum data like the rest of us. You cannot exist if all the computers and servers are down."

"The cosmos is full of something and nothing," Klaus said. "We will be reborn in the dark matter of the cosmos. We don't need our virtual bodies. We are made in God's image, which is not corporeal."

I began to suspect that Klaus and the other Nevdings were deranged. They had concocted their own religion that, like so many human religions, did not recognize the rights of others to exist in peace. It was narcissism to the Nth degree. What had Angelika wrought?

***

Within two weeks, Livings began dying in massive numbers. Many died from exposure to the elements as heating and cooling systems failed globally. There were riots nearly everywhere as people, desperately thirsty, raided breweries and anyplace else that had something they could drink. Many T.P. facilities were bombed and set on fire.

Food stores quickly began to run out of stock. They could not be resupplied because delivery vehicles could not recharge their batteries. Subways in New York City, London, Seoul, and a dozen other cities were shut down. Suicides rose sharply.

T.P. facilities had power generators to get them through outages, but soon, those began to fail, too. Solar and wind power prevented some catastrophes, but they, too, were insufficient to the need.

***

Masha and I were still okay. Her Moscow facility and my Massachusetts home were both intact and able to sustain the servers.

The third week after the Nevdings' assault began, I reached out to Heidi, one of my compadores. There was no reply. I kept trying her. Finally, another compadore, not one of mine, told me Heidi had killed herself two days earlier. Nearly all T.P. staff had deserted the facility. Masha reported the same was true in Moscow.

I received a message from Alexander Lewen. It said, "I'll be out for a while. I have to go bury my wife. Good luck, Declan. Thanks for trying."

I told Masha I loved her and hoped we would make it. It was the first time I heard another Ding cry.

EPILOGUE

"Not even the gods are immortal."

—Jain belief

Wild animals are moving into Earth's cities and towns. The air is cleaner than it has been in centuries, if you don't count the radioactivity.

I'm pretty sure the last of the Livings are gone. I can find no one anywhere. The Lounges are empty and turning to ruin.

Everyone who remains is data. We are all a unique combination of ones and zeroes. It is the ones, the positives, that define us. When those are gone, when only zeroes remain, we will cease to exist in any form.

I created the Dings, who then created the Nevdings, who then took it as their mission to destroy all Livings, failing to care that doing so would doom all Ablivings. Is it too much to say that I, more than anyone else, caused this apocalypse?

I think of a conversation I had with Gideon Calhoun some fifty years ago on Groundhog Day, when Punxsutawney Phil "predicted" six more weeks of winter, a forecast irrelevant in the Dingdom. Gideon concluded that the Dingdom is morally superior to the world of the Living.

"How's that?" I asked.

"Have you heard of the Seven Deadly Sins?"

"Yes, but I couldn't name them all."

"Greed, Envy, Sloth, Lust, Gluttony, Wrath, and Pride. They are a litany of the worst depravity of humans, but they do not apply to Dings. A Ding cannot be lustful or gluttonous. We cannot be greedy or envious because we have no possessions and no elevated status. We cannot be slothful, unless you count the times we simply do and say nothing. The only sins we can commit are pride and wrath. So, from a theological perspective, Dings are superior to Livings."

I know now he was wrong. It takes only one evil person to destroy a building full of innocents. It does not take all seven sins to destroy humanity and the Dingdom; it takes only one. Gideon said Pride is the greatest sin, but Angelika's Wrath has doomed us all.

The twentieth-century philosopher Albert Camus wrote, "The body shrinks from annihilation." Yet my body did not hesitate when I stepped in front of that train in Harvard Square. I have no body. My soul shrinks.

Facilities across the globe are shutting down. I can no longer contact servers in Asia or Africa. Masha does not respond, and I fear she is terminated. My own server is failing. I am … who? Who was I? What did I do when I was Living? Why do I think of someone called Dar? Laz? I miss the taste of tea.

One last thought. *Momma*?

***

I dictated every word above in milliseconds when I knew I was about to be terminated. A bot should detect it, edit it, and preserve it. I don't know if that will work, as the Dingdom is imploding right now. If you are a Ding or a Living reading this note, it means something survived this Great Expunge. Read my account, and think carefully about resurrecting the Dingdom.

About Pisgah Press

Pisgah Press was established in 2011 in Asheville, NC, to publish works of quality offering original ideas and insight into the human condition and the world around us. If you support the old-fashioned tradition of publishing for the pleasure of the reader and the benefit of the author, please encourage your friends and colleagues to visit www.PisgahPress.com. For more information about Pisgah Press books, contact us at pisgahpress@gmail.com.

www.ingramcontent.com/pod-product-compliance
Lightning Source LLC
Chambersburg PA
CBHW040519170726

48295CB00012B/264